D0975937

GABY, LOST AND FOUND

BY:
ANGELA CERVANTES

Scholastic Press / New York

Acknowledgments

This novel started out as my undercover plot to convince my husband that we needed to adopt a puppy from the animal shelter, but over time it's become so much more. I am grateful to the many people who helped me complete this book. Special thanks to Christine Taylor-Butler for inviting me to a writer's workshop where I'd meet my future kick-butt literary agent. You are so right, Christine: The universe works the way it should — bringing the right people together at the right time.

Mil abrazos to Adriana Dominguez Ferrari of Full Circle Literary Agency for believing in me and this story. *Muchisimas gracias* to my editor, Anna Bloom, and everyone at Scholastic for being my partners in the puppy plot.

Hugs to the Firehouse Five in Kansas City: Lisa Cindrich, Victoria Dixon, Tessa Elwood, Janet Johnson, and Jane True for the tireless edits and encouragement every step of the way. Fist bumps to my young editors: Alyssa, Carly, Claire, Riley, and Sofia, for being awesome.

Thanks to my friends and family who asked me, "How's the book going?" Your interest kept me going. *Muchos besitos* to my husband, Carlos Antequera, for my beautiful writing room. And you still owe me that puppy.

Most important, big hugs to all the Gabys out there. I hope I've done your story justice. Stay strong, *hermanitas*.

Con cariño,

Angela

Library of Congress Cataloging-in-Publication Data Available

ISBN 978-0-545-48945-4

10 9 8 7 6 5 4 3 2 1   13 14 15 16 17

Printed in the U.S.A. 23
First edition, August 2013
Book design by Nina Goffi

for my mom and dad, Pamela and Lorenzo Cervantes,
who gave me love and lots of books

Para mi mamá y papá, Pamela y Lorenzo Cervantes,
quienes me dieron amor y muchos libros

Chapter 1

A Siamese cat crouched on a tree branch, peering down at Gaby with brilliant blue eyes. It cried out. The cat was stuck in the tree in front of her house and, as luck would have it, she had on the nicest sweater she owned. Gaby pulled the cardigan sweater tighter around her. This was her last good school sweater until who-knows-when her father would have enough money to buy her a new one. The poor cat cried again. Gaby looked back at her small yellow house. If her mother were here, that cat would already be out of the tree and purring — safe and sound, in her mother's arms.

Mind made up, Gaby pulled off her sweater and tossed it onto her porch. "You're out of luck, *gato*!" she yelled. "My mom, master tree climber and cat rescuer, isn't back yet." She rolled up the sleeves of her white dress shirt. "But until she is, you got me." Gaby grasped the nearest branch and pulled herself up. "Gaby to the rescue."

The cat meowed.

"I *am* hurrying."

The last time Gaby had climbed the tree was when she and her best friend, Alma, had challenged the boys to a water-balloon fight last summer. Up high was the perfect spot for a full-blown assault on the boys below. Those guys never had a chance.

Gaby secured her feet and hands and climbed higher, until the cat was within arm's reach. "See? You aren't the only one who can climb." But then she looked down. Mistake number one.

She knew that the universal rule of tree climbing said don't ever, *ever* look down, but she couldn't help it. This was the highest she'd ever climbed. If she fell, she'd definitely end up looking like an Egyptian mummy. Gaby imagined herself bandaged from head to toe and sipping dinner through a straw.

Well, she'd just have to not fall. Simple as that. "Here, kitty, kitty!" she called out, the same way she had heard her mom call for stray cats hundreds of times. But this was no stray. The cat was too shiny. Too chubby. Around its neck, a rhinestone collar with gold charms sparkled. Someone loved that cat. She reached out toward it. "Almost got you." Mistake number two.

The cat arched its back and hissed.

Gaby pulled back, startled. "Nice teeth." She resettled on the branch, considering her options.

When Gaby was younger, she had seen her mom climb the same tree many times to rescue a cat. All the way up, her mom had giggled and sweet-talked the cat in Spanish. "*Que bonita eres gatita*. You're so pretty, little cat." Her mom told her that when dealing with cats you should speak softly and pick them up by the loose skin at the back of their neck, because that's how their mothers carried them. Her mom had always made it look so easy. Once she had the cat nestled against her chest, she would maneuver down through the branches, comforting the cat with kisses on the ears and soft words with rolling Spanish *r*'s like purrs. There were never any arched backs, hisses, or sharp teeth.

Gaby took a deep breath and reached out for the cat again. "It's okay, little kitty," she said sweetly. This time the cat latched on to her, digging its claws into her arm and shoulder. "Ooh, ouch!" She couldn't quite get it by the scruff of the neck like her mom had shown her, but at least she had the animal. That was progress. Now she just had to get down.

Without falling.

She held on to the cat and, with one free hand, made her way down the tree, branch by branch. She was halfway down when a loud, brash voice broke her concentration.

"Gaby, what are you doing up there?" Alma hollered.

"Taking a nap!" Gaby shouted back, careful to keep a tight grip on the tree and the cat.

"Be careful!"

"I'm always" — Gaby's foot slipped, but she quickly regained her foothold — "careful."

A faint squeak of metal signaled Marcos and Enrique pulling up on their bikes. Both of them were wearing their usual long white T-shirts and baggy basketball shorts. Between the branches, Gaby saw Enrique point up at her. Marcos flung his head of dark hair back, laughed, and clapped as if whatever Enrique had said was the funniest thing he'd ever heard. They were probably making a joke about her falling on her butt. "We're almost there, kitty," she crooned.

Finally, she swung her legs over the lowest branch and jumped down. The cat leaped out of her arms with a screech.

"You're welcome!" Gaby yelled as the cat scurried down the street. She inspected her shirt and pants. Her clothes were still intact, but her shoulder ached and her arm was covered in red welts.

Alma pulled a leaf out of Gaby's wavy brown hair. "Not very grateful, is she?"

"That's Mrs. Sepulveda's cat," Enrique said. He leaned his bike against the tree. "Whenever she opens her front door that cat takes off. One time she gave me five dollars to get it down from her roof. It almost ended my basketball career." Tall and skinny in an athletic way, Enrique played all the sports, but basketball was his favorite. He held the neighborhood record for most games of Horse won. "I still have the scars." He stuck out his long arm and twisted it to search his scabby elbow for the old wounds.

"Hey, watch this!" Marcos yelled from across the street. He showed off a no-hand wheelie on his red-and-silver low-rider bike, and then jumped the curb. He stopped a few inches from the girls. "Fa-Zam in your face!"

Gaby yawned. Alma closed her eyes and snored.

"That's cool," Marcos said. He got off his bike and walked it over to the porch. "I'll remember you both when I'm in Las Vegas performing daredevil stunts for millions of dollars."

"Millions? I can see your stunts for free on YouTube." Alma shook her dark curls. "If I were you, I'd stick to the palm reading. Now, *there's* a trick that won't paralyze you from the neck down." Gaby laughed and gave her a high five.

When Marcos wasn't doing wheelies on his bike, he believed he could see the future in the thin, splintered lines of the palm. He steadied his bike against Gaby's porch and sat down on the steps. "I know you only say that because you care." He brushed back a swatch of black hair from his hazel eyes and flashed both girls a smile. "Speaking of palm readings, anyone want one? I need the practice. Anyone?"

Alma busied herself with rewrapping her purple scarf around her neck and hummed. Enrique stared off into the tree as if it had suddenly spoken to him.

"Okay, okay." Gaby grabbed her sweater, tied it around her waist, and sat next to Marcos. "But I don't want to hear that I'm going to die before the age of thirty from a heart attack like you tell everyone."

Even though Marcos and Enrique were a year older than the girls, all four had been friends since they had training wheels on their bikes. As long as they could remember, Marcos had boasted that he was gifted with the power of palm reading. Some women in the neighborhood even paid him to read their palms.

"Tell me what we'll be doing for our sixth-grade service project."

"I'm a palm reader, not a psychic." Marcos took Gaby's hand. "Still, I might be able to help you . . . What are your choices?"

"An animal shelter or the City Harvest Center," Gaby answered.

"Both are lame." Alma rolled her eyes.

"Working with animals would be fun." Gaby shrugged. "That would be better than the City Harvest Center."

"Totally." Alma nodded.

Gaby passed her a slight smile. Ever since Gaby's mom was deported and her father had moved back into the house to take care of her, money had been tight. Everyone in the neighborhood knew that Gaby and her father were struggling, but only Alma knew that twice a month they went to the City Harvest Center to pick up food.

"What you got against free food for poor people?" Marcos chided.

"Nothing. It's just . . . it's just I . . ." Gaby stammered. She was on a first-name basis with the staff at the City Harvest Center. The minute she walked in the door it was, "Hey, Gaby, what's up?" At the center, she and her father picked up boxes filled with canned tuna, peanut butter, spaghetti, and toilet paper. Sometimes if the center had a special donation of cookies they'd throw in extra for Gaby. She never had the heart to tell them she didn't like sweets. She always took the extra cookies with a big smile and said thanks at least a hundred times before she left. Gaby was grateful for the Harvest Center. She just didn't want to go there with her classmates. "I'd rather take care of the animals. That's all."

"Hmmmm, the food pantry or an animal shelter, you say . . ." Marcos narrowed his hazel eyes and traced a line on Gaby's palm with his finger. Suddenly he lifted her hand to his nose and sniffed. "I smell kitty poop!"

Gaby yanked her hand away while he and Enrique laughed.

"You're ridiculous." Gaby glared at Marcos.

"My Uncle Junior and me took a box of puppies to a shelter once," Enrique said. "We found them by the Parkway Bridge. You know, where the sign is that says NO DUMPING?"

"Why do people do that? It's dangerous with all the cars and the woods." Gaby shook her head.

"My uncle says it's because people think that the animals will like living there. There's lots of birds, snakes, and mice to hunt," Enrique said.

"Or maybe they don't know about your house." Marcos pointed to the small white saucer on the bottom step.

When Gaby's mom had lived at home, she filled the saucer with food for the strays. Sometimes, it was leftover chicken from the evening's dinner. Other times it was slices of sandwich meat or oatmeal, anything she could spare, which wasn't a lot, but her mom always managed to find something. *Animales* depend on us to take care of them, she'd always tell Gaby. Every night, stray cats and dogs showed up on the porch as if a secret animal network had spread the word about the nice woman in the yellow house who feeds the strays.

One night, when Gaby's father still lived with them, he ran a skinny gray cat away from the porch. Her mom was heartbroken. It was the first time Gaby had heard her mom raise her voice to her father. "It's easy *para ti* to scare them off, but I've been that cat," she'd said. "I know how it feels to be the one looking for food and a safe place."

Gaby hadn't known what her mother meant at the time, but later her mom told her about the many nights she had slept outside and traveled on an empty stomach from her home country of Honduras to reach the United States.

That night, after cleaning the scratches on her arm, Gaby filled the small saucer on her porch with milk. It was all she had to spare. She checked the dining room table for a note from her father. It was covered with bills and newspapers, but nothing from him letting her know what time he'd be home. As usual, she made her bed on the couch, keeping the cordless phone next to her.

When she finally fell asleep, she dreamed there was a knock at the door. Her mom called to her.

"Gaby, it's me. I don't have my key, please let me in," she said.

In her dream, Gaby jumped from the couch and opened the door, but her mother wasn't there. Instead, the Siamese cat she'd rescued earlier gazed up at her. She'd recognize those blue eyes anywhere. When Gaby bent down to pick the cat up it swiped her face with its claws. Gaby cried out. She woke grasping her cheek.

Through the dark, she looked toward the front door. It was closed. No cat. No mom. Then she heard her father's voice. She sat up and saw him hunched over the dining room table with his back to her. She felt around for the cordless, but it was gone. Her father was whispering to someone on the phone. He mumbled something about money and about not wanting to risk something.

"Dad, who are you talking to?"

"Go to sleep, Gaby. It's late."

"Is it Mom?"

He quickly whispered good-bye to the caller and hung up.

"Dad?"

"Don't worry about it. Go to sleep." He stood up, went to his room, and closed the door behind him. Gaby got up, grabbed the phone from the table, and tucked it under her pillow.

chapter 2

Gaby almost tripped over her own feet as she and Alma slid into Mrs. Kohler's classroom. The school bell rang. It was Gaby's fault that she and Alma were almost late. Every morning for the last three months, she'd woken up tired. If it wasn't a bad dream about her mom that interrupted her sleep, it was her father coming home late. No matter how quiet he attempted to be, Gaby would hear him unlock the door, tiptoe past the couch, and close the door to his bedroom. And then there were the times — too many to count — that he'd bump into the dining room table or stub a toe in the dark and let out a painful series of curses. Serious curse words, that if repeated at St. Ann's would be grounds for expulsion.

Still, last night was different. All night she wondered who her father had been talking to and why he was being so secretive. If it was her mom why didn't he just say so? By the time she'd finally fallen asleep, it was morning. Gaby was still getting dressed when Alma's dad and Alma pulled up in their car to take her to school like they did every day. Thanks to Alma's father's precision driving, the girls made it to class on time . . . barely.

Mrs. Kohler frowned as they took their seats. "One more minute and you two would have missed the vote for our community project." Once the bell rang, Mrs. Kohler did not allow any late students into the classroom.

"Sorry, Mrs. Kohler," Gaby said, and then yawned.

If she slept in her bedroom Gaby would sleep better, but it wasn't an option. Ever since her mom had been deported to Honduras, Gaby had a reoccurring dream that her mom was knocking at the front door. It was just a dream, but Gaby didn't want to be tucked away in her bedroom, where she couldn't hear her mom at the front door when she finally returned home.

Gaby leaned toward Alma. "My dad is keeping something from me."

"Why am I not surprised?"

"I know." Gaby frowned. "Last night I woke up and heard him on the phone. He said something about money and not taking the risk again or something like that."

"Was he talking to your mom?"

"I thought about that, but then . . ." Gaby looked toward the front of the classroom. Mrs. Kohler was writing on the board. "They never talk to each other. She's still mad that he moved in after she left. She wanted me to stay with your family, you know? Not with him."

Alma nodded. "My mom and dad are still upset about that, too."

"She only talks to him if she absolutely has to. She's not all of a sudden going to have a secret middle-of-the-night conversation with him. Ever."

"He must be up to something." Alma tapped her fingers across her lips.

"Exactly!" Gaby pounded the desk with her hand.

Mrs. Kohler cleared her throat and gave Gaby and Alma a warning stare. The stare was part raised eyebrow and part pursed lip. Gaby was sure that all the teachers learned it their first year at St. Ann's from Sister Joan, principal and master of the warning stare.

The girls quieted. Alma gave Gaby a quick wink when Mrs. Kohler finally looked away. Alma enjoyed being the rebel. Even though she wore the same school uniform of khaki pants, white collared shirt, and navy blue cardigan as everyone else, Alma always managed to add something unique. In fourth grade, it was cowboy boots. The nuns at St. Ann's quickly put a stop to that. Last year, it was long gold necklaces. The nuns had a fit. This year, she wore a purple scarf loose around her neck. Even though the St. Ann's official school colors were navy blue and gold, so far the nuns had not objected.

Gaby was grateful for the school uniform. Even the stiff khaki pants. No matter how many times her father quit or lost a job, she still looked like all the other girls. So what if her shoes were from the Salvation Army store or her white shirts were paper thin and missing buttons? The cardigan sweater covered it.

"We will now vote to decide between two projects," Mrs. Kohler said. She floated around the rows of desks, handing out a paper about community service. "Our first option is Furry Friends Animal Shelter and our second is the City Harvest Center." All the girls cheered. Gaby bit her lower lip. Were her classmates applauding for the food pantry or the animal shelter? She hoped it was for the animal shelter.

It was bad enough that Gaby's classmates made sad puppy-dog faces whenever someone mentioned "illegal immigration" during social studies or religion class. If they went to the City Harvest Center, her classmates would know that she was so poor she depended on boxes of free food. This was not good. It wouldn't take long for that scoop of juicy news to get around school.

Three months ago, the factory her mom worked at was raided and all of the workers who could not show legal papers were hauled away. The story dominated the local news. Undocumented workers like her mom were held for weeks, and then sent back to their home countries. It didn't matter to the immigration agents that her mom shouldn't have even been at work that day. It had been her day off, but she was covering a shift for a coworker who had a sick baby. And it didn't matter to some of her classmates. Her mother's arrest and deportation was hot gossip. No one cared that Gaby's life was falling apart.

It made her not want to return to St. Ann's, but she had no choice. There wasn't any money to buy Gaby a ticket to Honduras. Plus, Gaby had been born in the United States. She didn't know Honduras. Still, the risks of moving to a new country had seemed easy at the time, compared to the stares and whispers she faced at school.

The City Harvest Center would be the same thing all over again. Even with Alma blocking the blows, once gossipy eighth graders like Dolores and Jan got started, the teasing would be unbearable. She could see it now: Dolores would stop her in the hallway and snidely ask, "Did you pick up your box from the center this month?" Maybe Dolores and Jan would leave canned food at her locker just as they had left pictures of Martian aliens taped on her locker months before. Gaby shuddered.

"Let's take a vote," Mrs. Kohler said.

Gaby tapped Alma's arm. "I'm voting for the sweet little dogs and cats."

"Said the girl with the sweet little scratches." Alma smirked.

"It's not that bad." Gaby rubbed her arms. "Besides, I'd happily save that cat again."

"Not me." Alma shook her head. "There are enough claws out with Dolores around. I don't need more!"

Gaby lowered her head. "I can't go to the Harvest Center. I just can't."

Alma gave her a knowing, sympathetic smile. "Don't worry. I got this." She stood up. "Mrs. Kohler and dear classmates, I would like to say that we should go to the Furry Friends Animal Shelter because even though I may not be a fan of stinky dog poop" — the classroom filled with giggles — "or itchy cat hair, I happen to know there are many animal lovers in this class."

"Thank you, Alma," Mrs. Kohler said. Alma remained standing. "Is there something else?"

"Well," she offered, "the animal shelter would be something different for us."

"Very good, Alma, but you do realize no one is contesting the animal shelter?"

"Oh . . . well, then I guess it makes no sense to mention that the eighth graders have to clean up a park for their community project. And the seventh graders are collecting pop cans. We have a chance to play with puppies. *Puppies.* Think about it, *chicas.* Let's stick it to the seventh and eighth graders and —"

"Alma Gomez!" Mrs. Kohler interrupted. "I think you've made your point."

So when the class voted, Gaby and Alma — along with the entire classroom — raised their hands in support of Furry Friends Animal Shelter. Gaby smiled at her best friend, relieved. "Marcos was right, Alma. He predicted we'd go to the shelter."

"Yeah, itchy-scratchy-cat-hair-all-over-our-clothes, here we come." Alma brushed invisible cat hair off her purple scarf.

ChAPteR 3

Furry Friends Animal Shelter was located in a part of Kansas City that neither Gaby nor Alma knew.

"Fancy *schmancy*." Gaby nudged Alma. "That's the fifth slug bug I've seen."

"I've counted two yoga studios and four coffee shops," Alma said.

When the school bus pulled up to the shelter, all the girls hopped out and pressed down their school shirts. A tall, lanky man dressed in blue jeans and a black *Star Wars* T-shirt emerged from the building.

"Welcome!" he yelped, striding down the sidewalk toward them. As he approached, his hands flew up over his head like he was on a roller coaster. "Welcome to Furry Friends!"

Gaby couldn't take her eyes off him. "If he had a tail, it'd be wagging," she whispered to Alma.

He had a long ponytail of black hair, thick dark eyebrows that hovered over brown eyes, and a goatee. Both his arms were covered with colorful tattoos, and a silver stud sparkled from one earlobe. Gaby liked him at once.

"I'm not sure whether I should shake his hand or put a leash on him," Alma said.

"Hi, Dr. Villalobos, I am Mrs. Kohler. And these students are the brightest in our school." Mrs. Kohler's tiny hands gestured toward the girls. The tall man, who looked younger and cooler than any doctor Gaby had ever met, scratched his chin and took a long look at them.

"That is phenomenal! Good afternoon, sixth graders. I'm Dr. V. Are you young ladies ready to meet some furry friends?"

The girls answered yes, but apparently not loudly enough for him. He howled, "Ready to meet some furry friends?"

Mrs. Kohler nodded at the girls and they screamed "*YES!*" at the top of their lungs.

"Right on! Let's go!" He punched the air with his fist and led them to the lobby. He stopped at the front desk, where an older woman with red hair and black-rimmed glasses sat shuffling through papers. "Daisy, these are our volunteers from St. Ann's. Everyone, this is the lovely Daisy, shelter director!"

Gaby liked how Daisy wore her long hair at the nape of her neck like an orange roll without the frosting. Daisy gave them a thumbs-up. "Glad to have you ladies here."

The students followed Dr. V. into a large room where dozens of dogs of every size and breed jumped, barked, and yelped in their cages. He placed his hands like a bullhorn around his mouth and yelled over the ruckus, "Aren't they fantastic?"

Alma covered her ears with her hands. Gaby chuckled.

"Beware the next room. It's full of fluffy kittens and cool cats that will steal your heart with one meow."

Walking from the dog room to the cat room was like the rainbow after a thunderstorm. The room was painted turquoise blue. Hot pink scratching posts, yellow pillows, and balls of yarn of every color were lined up on high shelves. An assortment of stuffed toy rats and mice lay defeated on the tiled floor, looking like they'd seen better days. A couple of cats lounging near a large window looked back at the girls and yawned. Kittens stuck their paws out of their cages and mewed as the girls moved from one cage to another squealing, "Look at this kitty!" and, "Aw, this one is so cute!"

Dr. Villalobos opened a cage. "Go ahead. Hold them. Human contact is important to help shelter pets become sociable and more adoptable."

Gaby didn't hesitate. She took a small yellow kitten named Lemon from its cage. She ran her hand over its soft back. "Poor thing, I bet it hates being caged up." Just then the kitten clasped its small paws around Gaby's pigtail as if it'd caught a snake. Gaby winced as it pulled and chewed her hair.

"Ew! Ouch! It won't let go!" Gaby cried out. Alma worked fast to detach the cat's claws and tiny teeth from Gaby's thick brown hair. When she got the two separated, she returned Lemon to its cage.

"What was that you were saying about the 'poor thing'?" Alma grinned.

"Not funny." Gaby smoothed down her hair and pouted.

Dr. Villalobos motioned for the girls to follow him into the veterinarian clinic. Once inside the clinic, he pulled a skinny cat out of a cage. The cat was like no cat Gaby had ever seen. She was gray, tan, and white with black stripes that streamed from her forehead and down her back. Above the cat's bright green eyes was a dark M. It was the sign of a true tabby. Gaby was sure that the M stood for marvelous, magical, magnificent . . .

The cat cried out.

"Shush, it's all right." Dr. Villalobos swayed with the cat like a father soothing a fussy baby. "This is Feather. Who wants to hold her?"

Gaby's hand flew up. Alma gave her an incredulous look. Gaby wasn't having much luck with cats lately. The stray from yesterday had left her with red welts and a bad dream, and Lemon had just tried to eat her hair. Still . . . she couldn't resist.

Dr. Villalobos passed Feather to Gaby. She was stunned by how light the cat was. She glided her hand over its fur. The cat's ribs poked out like the handlebars on Marcos's bike.

"Why is she so skinny?" Gaby asked.

"Feather was abandoned at a rest stop. I named her Feather because when she came in, she was as light as a feather. If you can believe it, she's actually gained weight."

"Someone just abandoned her?" Gaby said. The cat purred deep and low against her chest.

Dr. Villalobos nodded. "The highway patrol said she was sitting at a picnic table as if she was waiting for someone. She's also declawed, which means she was definitely some-one's pet." He took Feather from Gaby and showed the girls Feather's clawless front paws. The cat let out a soft meow and reached back toward Gaby. Gaby's heart jumped. All the girls sighed.

"Wow! She likes you." Dr. Villalobos said. He put Feather back into her cage. "You two can visit later. Right now, it's time to play outside with the wolves!"

While her classmates swarmed past her to head outside, Gaby stopped at the doorway and looked back at Feather. The small cat locked eyes with her and meowed.

"I'll be back," Gaby answered.

The shelter's backyard was lined with large pine trees, and along one side of the yard there were a number of large pens that held two dogs each. The dogs jumped wildly. Their barking became louder when Daisy brought out a few dogs from inside the shelter. Dr. Villalobos explained the play-time rules and instructed the girls to dispose of dog droppings in a specific trash can.

"I knew it! This is going to get bad," Alma said. She wrinkled her nose. "Dr. Villalobos?" she shouted. "What if the poop is slimy and we can't pick it up?" A white-toothed grin took over Dr. V's entire face. He even chuckled. Alma pressed on. "You know what I mean, right?"

"Yeah, that slimy poop can be quite a sticky situation. In that case, you should grab the big shovel over there and scoop it up. And please let us know because that's a sign that the dog is sick or has dietary issues, and we need to fix that."

Gaby elbowed Alma. "I know what we can do — quick, let's make friends with a small dog because their stuff will be . . . you know, smaller." The girls spotted a small black-and-white terrier. The dog was chewing on a stuffed purple bear.

"He seems harmless, huh?" Alma said. The terrier looked up at her with wet brown eyes. "Don't look at me like that," she snapped. "You're cute, but you're not that cute." She sat down on the grass, grabbed the stuffed toy, and began a game of tug-of-war with the dog. The feisty terrier jerked the stuffed toy and Alma from left to right. The dog growled and Alma grunted.

"I think you've met your match." Gaby giggled.

"So what do you think about this place?"

"Cool, but I'd like to take care of the sick animals, too." Gaby looked toward the clinic. "Like Feather." Daisy and Dr. Villalobos were at the clinic entrance, deep in conversation. Whatever they were discussing made Daisy drop her shoulders and Dr. Villalobos lower and shake his head. Gaby hoped whatever it was had nothing to do with Feather.

Chapter 4

Before the girls left the shelter for the day, Dr. Villalobos sat them in a circle outside on the grass. "Every day, shelters like ours accept thousands of dogs and cats brought in by animal control or people like you. Here at Furry Friends, these animals get a second chance to be loved and find a good home," he said. "Unfortunately, right now our shelter is completely full. That means we can't accept any more."

"Thousands?" Gaby asked.

Dr. Villalobos nodded. "I have hundreds of stories about the dogs and cats here at the shelter. Some really sad stories, but they were lucky to wind up at our shelter." He paused and looked back at the cage that housed Cinder, the rottweiler pup. "Cinder was found by police behind an abandoned house. She was tied with a thick chain to a post. Poor thing had scratched off all the fur around her neck trying to free herself. Her ear and tail had been ripped, possibly in a fight with another dog, and she was severely dehydrated and flea infested."

The mere mention of fleas made Gaby scratch her neck. She looked back at Cinder. Earlier, she had noticed that whenever any of the girls approached Cinder's cage, the pup backed away and whimpered. Now Gaby understood why.

"How about that little black-and-white dog? What's his story?" Alma asked.

"That's Spike. He was found near the highway. From what animal control told us, Spike was running in and out of traffic barking at cars," Dr. Villalobos said. "He's lucky he wasn't hit."

Alma shook her head. "That dog is nuts."

"Spike was adopted twice, but both times the families brought him back to the shelter complaining that he was too wild. I'm afraid if Spike doesn't change he'll never know the joy of a real home and family."

Alma gulped. "That's not right."

"Poor Spike," Gaby said.

"Many of the cats were dumped here as newborns," Dr. Villalobos continued. "So they're like my babies." All the girls sighed. "People don't know what to do when their pet has a litter so they put them in a box and leave them at our door, which is still better than dumping them in the woods or open fields."

"In our neighborhood," Alma said, "people dump their pets under the Parkway Bridge. It's a big problem."

"So then you know what I'm talking about." Dr. V. nodded. "I'm hoping you ladies can promote the shelter so that we can find homes for the animals here and open up space for other homeless animals."

Gaby raised her hand. "Can you put these stories on your website and on flyers?"

Dr. Villalobos's face brightened. "I've never had time to do that. Maybe you ladies could help me with it?"

"Gaby could write them," Alma said. Gaby jabbed her with her elbow.

"Yes, she is a very creative writer," Mrs. Kohler spoke up. Gaby peered over at Mrs. Kohler, who winked at her. "She will do a superb job."

Gaby dropped her head back, exasperated. Could she really write these stories?

"Sweet! Our very own shelter scribe. How perfect is that?" Dr. Villalobos bobbed his head. "Too perfect."

Alma whispered to Gaby, "His tail is definitely wagging now."

Gaby glared at her. "Shelter scribe?"

"Catchy, isn't it?"

Gaby rolled her eyes.

By the end of the talk, the class had planned an entire adoption campaign for the shelter. They'd take new photos of each dog and cat for flyers and the website. A team of girls, led by Alma, would train dogs like Spike to be less wild and more adoptable. For the grand finale, they'd have an open house to bring people into the shelter.

"We could call our open house Barkapalooza," Dr. Villalobos said.

The girls responded with polite smiles and a few claps.

He howled, "What do you think, ladies? I want to hear some noise!"

The girls screamed at the top of their lungs and Dr. Villalobos led them in a loud chant of "Barkapalooza."

At school, the girls were always being told to "keep it down" or "be quiet please, young ladies." Dr. Villalobos seemed to prefer that they make as much noise as possible. Gaby liked that about him.

As her classmates continued the chant all the way to the

bus, Gaby pulled her notebook from her book bag. She thumbed through the blank pages. If her mom was around, she would tell Gaby to give *todo su corazón* and nothing less than her whole heart to help the animals, but Gaby had no idea what to write about them. Plus, there were a lot of dogs and cats in the shelter! She couldn't write stories for all of them, could she? There weren't enough words, adverbs, or adjectives in the dictionary to make a bunch of lost cats and unwanted dogs sound appealing. Were there?

On the inside of the notebook cover, she wrote her mother's words: "*Animales* depend on us to take care of them." It wasn't much, but it was true, and it was a start.

CHAPTER 5

The next day at school, Gaby received special permission from Mrs. Kohler to leave during silent reading time and go to the cafeteria to write profiles. She doodled an image of Spike chewing on his stuffed panda. Next, she sketched a picture of Feather with a bold M above her almond-shaped eyes. Still, no words came to her. There were so many dogs and cats that needed homes: Pouncer, Lemon, Cinder, Puck, Atticus, Secret, Snowflake, Bonita, Spike, and Feather. If the list never stopped, where was she supposed to start?

Frustrated, Gaby looked around the cafeteria. It was mostly empty except for the kitchen staff cleaning up after lunch and a group of eighth graders studying at the far end, near the stage. When she'd spotted them there, she considered going back to class, but she needed to get away to stir up her creative juices. She chose the table farthest away from the older girls. Any farther and she would have been outside in the teachers' parking lot.

The St. Ann's cafeteria also served as the school's theater. It was where they held their annual Christmas program, "Christmas Around the World." The nuns burned cinnamon-scented candles to hide the cafeteria smell and each class presented on how Christmas was celebrated in a country of their choice. This year, the sixth graders had covered Mexico. Alma's mom made Mexican sweet bread called *conchas*. And the class ended the presentation on Mexico by breaking a star-shaped piñata filled with pennies and Tootsie Rolls.

Gaby's class had wanted to present on Honduras in honor of Gaby's mom, but Gaby had told them to wait until next Christmas. By then, she said, her mom would be home. She and her mom could prepare tamales made with plantain leaves, *arroz con leche*, and hot chocolate for everyone. It would be a true Honduran feast! And from center stage, Gaby imagined that she and Alma would lead the entire cafeteria in singing "Silent Night" in Spanish. *Noche de paz . . . noche de amor . . .*

Next thing Gaby knew, Dolores and Jan were scowling at her from across the room. Gaby looked away, confused. What did she do? Then she realized that while she was staring off toward the stage, deep into "Silent Night," it must have seemed like she was staring at them. Dolores and Jan were the ones who had given her the hardest time after her mom was arrested. She was certain it was Dolores who had left pictures of skinny, slant-eyed, cone-headed green space aliens on her locker. And if she passed Dolores and her sidekick, Jan, in the hallway, they'd cough "illegal," or other awful names not worth repeating. Those had been some of the worst days of Gaby's life.

Trying hard to focus on the blank sheet of paper in front of her, Gaby felt their eyes burn into her skin. Were they still looking at her? She glanced up in time to see Rosa, one of the most popular girls in school, say something to them. The scowls stopped. Whatever Rosa said must have been severe, because Dolores and Jan turned back to their books and the rest of the girls followed. Gaby was relieved.

At the shelter, Lemon, the small yellow kitten that attacked her hair, would jump and hide under its blanket whenever a dog barked. That's how Gaby felt whenever Dolores and Jan looked her way. She picked up her pen and began a list of other things she had observed about the young male cat. Lemon arrived as a newborn to the shelter with a litter of siblings. If you had long hair, beware! Lemon was bound to chew on it like it was spaghetti. Still, he was a sweet kitten that loved to be scratched behind the ears. Gaby decided it was best to leave out the hair-chewing bit. Next, she wrote a list of things that were yellow like Lemon. A gold coin. A field of wheat. The sun. An ear of corn. Within minutes, she had finished her first profile.

LEMON

Don't let the name fool you. Lemons may be sour, but I'm as sweet as they come. I am a three-month-old male cat that came to the shelter with my siblings when we were just a few weeks old. I am as shiny yellow as a gold coin in your pocket or an ear of corn on your plate. I like to start my day with a saucer of milk and end it with a good scratch behind the ears. No need to add sugar to this lemon! Please visit me at Furry Friends Animal Shelter and take me home today!

CHAPTER 6

"My dad's here," Gaby gasped. Her father's old blue truck was parked in the front of Alma's house.

"Yeah," Mrs. Gomez said from the driver's seat. "We invited him over to discuss things."

Gaby knew exactly what those "things" were. "Things" meant Gaby's living arrangements. When everyone realized that Gaby's mom was not going to be released by immigration and that, in fact, she was going to be deported to Honduras, Alma's family offered to take care of Gaby full-time. After all, Gaby had never been close to her father. Her parents never married, and her dad moved out when Gaby was in elementary school. After that, her father only came around twice a year: Gaby's birthday and Christmas. Sometimes he barely made those occasions. But when he heard about Gaby's mom being deported, he decided to move back into the house. It was in Gaby's best interest, he said, that she stay in her home with family.

For Gaby, it might as well have been a stranger off the street moving in. He knew nothing about her or how to take care of a daughter. Gaby learned to take care of herself. She went to bed when she wanted, woke herself up for school, combed and styled her hair, made her own breakfast — usually instant hot chocolate and a slice of toast with peanut butter — and cleaned up any mess her father left in the house. Weekends were spent at Alma's house, where she had her own bed and did laundry.

Inside, Gaby's dad and Mr. Gomez sat at the kitchen table. Alma's father had always gotten along with Gaby's father and even helped him find work with local construction projects or within his own company, but no job lasted long. Gaby's dad complained that his bosses were jerks and everyone around him was a "nut job."

Gaby sat across from her father at the table. "I didn't hear you come home last night or see you this morning," she said. "What time did you get home?"

Her father ran his hands along his unshaven face and looked down. She wondered if anyone meeting them both for the first time would even suspect that they were father and daughter. He was blond with blue eyes and she had her mother's dark eyes and wavy brown hair.

"Nah, got off work late last night, decided it made no sense to drive all the way home only to turn right around." He rotated his head until his neck popped. "I slept in the truck."

Gaby caught Alma exchange a glance of disbelief with her mom. She felt a lump in her throat. She was used to her father's dismissive answers and excuses for coming home late, forgetting that she needed food, and not paying the electricity bill, but still, it embarrassed her a little. Gaby searched his face for a sign of remorse until he looked up and gave her a slight apologetic smile from under his ball cap. She lowered her head and decided not to say anything else.

"Mr. Howard, did Gaby tell you about our volunteer project at school?" Alma interrupted the tense silence.

Gaby's father took a swig from his glass of lemonade. "No, what volunteer project?"

"How could you not know, Jeff!" Alma's mother laughed. "You had to sign a permission slip."

His face contorted like he was trying to remember signing a permission slip. Gaby shot a worried look at Alma. For an entire week, she had left the permission slip on the table. He never signed it. On the day it was due, Gaby had no choice but to have Marcos forge her father's name.

"It's our school's required community service," Gaby said. "I'm writing profiles for all of the cats and dogs at an animal shelter. Would you like to hear one?" Gaby dug into her book bag and pulled out her notebook. She was anxious to get his mind off the permission slip. "I can read one —"

"Maybe later. I got to get going." Her father got up from the table.

"Already?" Gaby asked.

"I got this job, Gaby. And it's my turn to drive the guys tonight."

Gaby frowned. She had no idea who these "guys" were. She had no clue where he was working or what he was doing all day and night. He never bothered to tell her, and she'd stopped asking.

"That's actually why we wanted to talk, Jeff." Mr. Gomez stood up, too. "It's been three months and we know you're trying your best, but maybe you've changed your mind about allowing Gaby to stay with us full-time until things are more stable for you. What do you think?"

Gaby's father tugged his cap like he wished he could cover his entire face with it.

"You know I appreciate the offer. Heck, I appreciate everything you guys do for Gaby. But I think we're doing fine. Right, Gaby?" He shrugged.

She stared down at her notebook and unraveled the coil that held the pages in place. "Yeah, but . . ."

Her father shook his head. "I mean it's not ideal that your mom isn't here to take care of you, but she calls. You guys talk. You're doing okay."

Gaby swallowed hard. She wished she had the courage to tell her father that she wanted to stay with Alma's family. It *was* what she wanted, wasn't it? Just until her mom returned home?

"Well, we can talk about this later. I got to go." Her father fiddled with his keys. "I know I don't have to tell you to stay out of trouble, but stay out of trouble, Gaby." He pressed a five-dollar bill into her hand and patted her head. Gaby winced and stuffed the flimsy bill into her front pocket. Good thing she got free lunch at school. Five dollars wouldn't go far.

As Alma's parents walked her father to the door, Gaby opened her notebook. "That went well," she scoffed. She regretted not telling him that she wanted to stay with Alma's family. Gaby clicked her pen and wrote her name at the top of a blank page. "Maybe I should write an adoption flyer for myself."

"Hmmmmm," Alma said. "Something like this: 'Eleven-year-old St. Ann's scholar, loves gold glitter, math and science class —'"

"Looking for a home where I can have a cat like Feather and a —" Gaby stopped writing. She drew a breath and held it, staring down at the three-letter word she had scribbled. She wasn't looking for a new mom. She had a mom. And once her mom came home, there would be no more being left alone at night or forging permission slips. And especially no more sleeping on the couch with the phone under her pillow. Things would be back to normal as soon as her mom was home. She exhaled finally and scratched out "a mom" with her pen.

"What's wrong?" Alma asked.

"Nothing, I was just thinking I could sprinkle gold glitter all over my profile for added bling."

"Are you sure?"

"Yeah, you're right, maybe silver glitter would be better." Gaby shut her notebook.

After a few seconds, the girls heard Marcos and Enrique at the front door, asking Alma's mom for permission to visit. Alma double-rolled her eyes. Marcos and Enrique always tried to be polite around Alma's parents, but the girls knew better. These were boys who cursed while playing Xbox and talked smack on the basketball court.

"Quick, play dead! Maybe they'll go away." Alma slumped in her chair, closed her eyes, and stuck out her tongue. Gaby followed.

"The boys are here." Alma's mom ushered Enrique and Marcos into the kitchen. "Stop playing dead and be nice," she giggled.

"Hide your jewelry, Mom!" Alma sprang up.

Marcos pulled Alma's long ponytail and mocked her. "Hide your jewelry, Mom."

Before leaving the kitchen, Alma's mom put a bowl of grapes on the table. Enrique and Marcos grabbed fistfuls and devoured them.

"You guys are about as well trained as the dogs at the shelter," Alma said.

"Alma, have any dogs bitten you for being mean yet?" Enrique bared his teeth and growled.

She growled back.

"What are you guys writing?" Marcos popped some grapes in his mouth.

"I'm writing profiles for the dogs and cats at the shelter," Gaby said. "Want to see one?" She flipped through her notebook, stopped on the profile for Secret, and slid it to him. Secret was a kitten that hid its food and toys under its blanket as if trying to keep them from the other cats. When these things were discovered by the staff, Secret's ears perked up in surprise as if he was saying, "How on earth did that get there?"

Marcos wiped his mouth with his hand, grabbed the notebook, and stood up. "And now it's time for a story about a cat named Secret," he said in a phony high-pitched British accent. Enrique and Alma laughed as Marcos began. Gaby shook her head. This was not going to be good.

SECRET

I am a healthy four-month-old kitten with long, silky black fur and white paws. I came to Furry Friends Animal Shelter with four of my siblings when we were just born. I'm the only one left to be adopted. Here at the shelter, I love to meow early in the morning. It's my special way of saying "hello!" My favorite toy this week is a long peacock feather, which I've hidden in a secret place. Shush, don't tell anyone! Visit me at Furry Friends Animal Shelter and I'll reveal all my secrets to you!

When Marcos finished, Gaby snatched her notebook from him. "You're never allowed to read my profiles again."

"Suit yourself." Marcos shrugged. "Do they have any big, vicious dogs that can be trained to kill zombies?"

"Stop being dumb." Alma shook her head. "Most of the animals there were abused and abandoned. They're not vicious. Of course, I found the smelliest and wildest mutt in the shelter." Alma took out her cell phone and showed them Spike's photo. "I'm going to train him to be the best-behaved dog in the world."

"Train him to kill zombies and my Uncle John-John will give you fifty dollars for him." Enrique smirked.

Alma rolled her eyes. "Not happening."

"There is a cat there that's all skin and bones," Gaby said. "She's sick. Right, Alma?"

"Yeah, they named her Feather because when she was brought to the shelter, she was as light as one."

"Well, if she's real sick," Marcos said, "the shelter will put her to sleep, you know."

"Dr. V. never mentioned anything about putting cats to sleep," Gaby protested.

"Earth to Gaby, that's what they do at those shelters," Marcos said, earning a sharp kick from Alma under the table. "Ouch! That's what happens — I'm just sayin'." Rubbing his leg, he glared at Alma. "You don't scare me."

Enrique pulled his long legs up onto his chair to avoid a kick. "You totally scare me, Alma, but Marcos is right. If that cat is seriously sick, they'll put it to —" Alma pinched his arm. "Ouch!" He yelped.

Gaby chewed a fingernail and looked over at Alma with alarm.

"Don't listen to them, Gaby." Alma raised her finger to make her point. "The shelter is called 'Furry Friends,' not 'Dead Furry Friends.'"

The boys erupted into snickers and snorts.

"Yeah, that would be an excellent name for an animal shelter, Alma," said Marcos. "Too bad they didn't think of that." Marcos stuck his tongue out at her.

"Such a nice ring . . . Dead Furry Friends Animal Shelter . . . so warm and comforting," added Enrique.

Alma crossed her arms. "Ignore them, Gaby," she said. "They have no clue."

Gaby didn't say anything more, but she was big-time worried. Would Dr. Villalobos put the sick animals to sleep to make room for others? Sick animals like Feather? That night, when Gaby said her prayers on the couch, she asked God to bless her mom and to help her save all of the animals at the shelter.

ChAPTER 7

Furry Friends Animal Shelter bustled with excitement. A couple had arrived to adopt a cat. The girls took the cats out of their cages one by one to show the couple. Pouncer, a small yellow kitten, loved to sit on the window ledge and swat at flies. Secret, the fluffy black kitten with the white paws, loved peacock feathers. Coco, the brown-and-white cat, purred whenever classical music played. As the couple pet and played with each feline presented to them, Gaby approached them.

Mr. Villalobos had told her that older cats usually spent their whole lives in shelters without ever having a real home because people preferred kittens. This saddened Gaby.

"How would you feel about an older cat that goes wild for catnip?" she asked the couple.

"Goes wild for catnip, you say?" The man pushed his glasses up on his nose.

"Yes, but not too wild. Older cats, in general, are better behaved," Gaby added.

"You obviously don't know my wife very well." He smirked. His wife giggled and pressed a loose strand of silver hair behind her ear.

"What Gaby means is that mature cats don't run around all crazy like these kittens," Alma said. As if on cue, Pouncer leaped out of one of the girls' arms and tackled a tissue on the floor. After a few seconds, strands of tissue dangled from Pouncer's mouth. "See what I mean?" The couple raised their eyebrows and nodded.

It was the signal Gaby needed to grab Willow, an eight-year-old cat with intense blue eyes and a dark gray coat.

"Look at old blue eyes!" The man took Willow from Gaby. He ran his hands over Willow's head and back. The cat let out a soft, satisfied mew. The couple exchanged a big smile.

"I think you guys are a purrrr-fect match!" Gaby clasped

her hands. Alma gave her a thumbs-up. That cat was as good as gone.

After Daisy helped the new owners complete adoption papers, the girls ran outside to see them off. Dr. Villalobos and Gaby were the last two still waving until the couple's car was no longer in view.

"That cat is off to a brand-new start!" Dr. Villalobos beamed.

"One down, Dr. V.," she said. They walked to the back of the shelter together, where her classmates were playing with the dogs.

"With your profiles,"— he pointed at the notebook she carried under her arm —"maybe we'll be waving *adios* every day," he said. "Whose profile are you working on now?"

"I'd like to write one for Feather, but I need to spend some time with her to —"

"About Feather . . ." Dr. V. interrupted. "You might want to consider another cat or dog."

Gaby stopped walking. "What? Why? Is she okay?"

Dr. Villalobos turned to face her. "She may not be adoptable after all. Maybe you can write about Finch or Bonita?"

"Whenever I was sick, my mom used to sing to me in Spanish. It helped. I could sing for Feather."

Dr. Villalobos put his hand on Gaby's shoulder. "Good idea, but it's nothing like that." He started to walk away.

"Dr. Villalobos!" Gaby shouted, stopping Dr. V. in his tracks.

He stepped toward her. "Something wrong, Gaby?"

Gaby didn't realize how loud she'd yelled until she noticed that her classmates and even a few dogs were staring at her. She cleared her throat. "Sorry." She lowered her voice. "It's just there's no reason to put Feather to sleep. She's a good cat. If I could adopt her, I would right now."

Dr. V. crossed his arms across his chest and smiled.

"It's just my dad doesn't like cats. And my mom . . . well, it's a long story, but I don't think you should be putting cats to sleep. That's all."

"Gaby, you got it all wrong. Furry Friends is a no-kill animal shelter. We don't put any of our animals to sleep."

Gaby exhaled. "Oh . . . then why can't I write Feather's profile?"

"I got a call from a man looking for his cat. He described a cat exactly like Feather."

"He wants to claim her? But you said her owners left her at a rest stop. What kind of person leaves their cat and then wants it back weeks later?"

He patted her shoulder and smiled. "I knew I had the right person working on these profiles. I could tell by how you held Feather that first day that you were a natural animal lover."

"I learned it from my mom. She loves animals, too."

"Well, I'm counting on you to keep writing those pro-files, okay?" He winked at her and walked toward the clinic.

"Poor Feather," Gaby whispered. It wasn't fair. Feather deserved better than people who left her at a rest stop. She marched after Dr. V. to tell him so when Alma called her name, interrupting her mission. Alma was sitting on the grass with Spike and a brown pug/beagle mix named Puck. The two dogs stopped gnawing on each other's ears and looked up as Gaby approached.

Alma looked concerned about the conversation she'd just seen between Gaby and Dr. V.

"Are you okay, Gaby?"

"I asked Dr. V. about putting animals to sleep like Marcos said last night," Gaby explained.

"You're listening to Marcos now?" Alma grabbed her head with her hands. "Marcos thinks he's going to make a living jumping his bike through fiery hoops in Las Vegas."

"I know, I just had to know for sure."

"What did Dr. V. say?"

"He said the shelter was a no-kill shelter."

"Feel better?"

"Sort of." Gaby sat down on the grass. She still didn't like the idea of Feather returning to her former owners. Anyone who abandoned their pet like that shouldn't be allowed to reclaim it so easily.

"Good. Check out what I taught Spike and Puck." Alma called both dogs. "Sit," Alma ordered. Both dogs sat up. Alma's voice was so powerful that even Gaby sat up straighter. "Shake hands." Puck and Spike both raised a paw.

"Wow, Alma! How did you teach them so fast?" Gaby shook their paws. "Nice to meet you, Mr. Puck. *Mucho gusto,* Mr. Spike!"

"Obviously, I've had a lot of practice training Enrique and Marcos." Alma picked up Puck. He surprised her with a few quick licks that went up her nose. "So gross!" She flinched and put him down fast. She wiped her nose with her sleeve.

For a minute, Gaby forgot about her conversation with Dr. V. and laughed.

"You should write your next profile on Puck so that he can lick someone else's nose," Alma said.

Gaby opened her notebook. Puck sat at her feet and gazed up at her with wide, bulging eyes and a wagging tongue. Gaby hoped he wasn't planning to lick her nostrils, too.

"Don't get any ideas, Puck." She turned away, clicked her pen, and wrote. If Puck could talk, he'd probably recite poems about kisses, squeaky toys, and warm breezes.

PUCK

Hi, my name is Puck! I'm a one-year-old male brown pug/beagle mix that likes kisses! Some of my favorite things, besides smooches, are squeaky toys and long walks. I love to play with children. My future life plans include sticking my head out your car window to enjoy the breeze, giving you kisses every day, and making you the happiest dog owner ever! Visit Furry Friends Animal Shelter and take me home today!

CHAPTER 8

The next day, Gaby had put the last slice of bread they had into the toaster when her mom called.

"What's for breakfast, *princesa*?"

Gaby gulped hard. If her mom knew that Gaby's father wasn't home and that she had nothing in the house to eat but toast and a packet of hot chocolate, she'd freak. Gaby didn't want to add to her worries. Her mom had more important things to focus on — like traveling hundreds of miles to get back home.

"Scrambled eggs, turkey bacon, waffles, and orange juice."

"*¡Que rico!* Sounds delicious! I'm glad to hear your dad is taking good care of you. I was worried. So everything is okay?"

"Yes. Where are you calling from, Mom?"

"I'm at work."

Gaby sighed loudly. "I thought you'd be on your way home by now. You haven't called in a while so I thought maybe you were traveling and couldn't get to a phone . . ." Gaby's voice choked. Sometimes during Mrs. Kohler's long lectures, Gaby would look out the classroom window and imagine her mom making her way through Honduras, Guatemala, and Mexico by train and then walking across the Mexico-United States border with no problems. Her mother's perfect English and bright smile would convince the border agents that she belonged on this side. Just like that, her mom would be home and they'd never be separated again.

"I'm sorry, *princesa*. I've been working day and night trying to earn more money. Crossing is more dangerous than when I did it fourteen years ago. I need to hire a coyote to help me make the journey, and the good ones with experience demand more money. You understand, right?"

Coyotes were men paid to smuggle people across the U.S. border. It was a fitting name. Real coyotes traveled in packs and were nocturnal animals. These men would also lead a pack of people, like her mom, across Honduras, Guatemala, Mexico, and finally over the U.S. border, under the cover of night.

Gaby squeezed her eyes closed. "I just want you to come home like you promised."

"I know, Gaby. I miss you so much."

"I miss you more," Gaby whispered. She wished she were a powerful wizard that could wave a wand and have her mom instantly back at her side.

"*No llores, mi princesa.* Please."

Gaby let the tears stream down her cheek. Why wipe them away? It didn't stop anything. Not the bad dreams. Not the bullying from Dolores and Jan at school. Not the long days that passed without her mom.

"When do you think you'll have enough?"

"I don't know, Gaby. My aunt is sick, so I've taken over her work at the market on weekends, but it's still not enough. I don't want you to worry about that, though. Let me worry about the money. Tell me something new that's going on in your life."

Gaby pulled on a thick strand of her hair and twisted it. "Well . . . I heard Dad on the phone the other night whispering to someone about money. Maybe you could ask him for some."

"Gaby, you shouldn't listen in on your dad's phone conversations."

"At first, I thought it might be you, but you don't call that late."

"Don't give it one more thought. Tell me something good to keep me strong."

"There is nothing good."

"There must be something, *princesa*."

Gaby thought about Feather. "Our class is volunteering at an animal shelter."

"Oh, Gaby!" Her mom squealed. "That's great!"

"I'm in charge of writing stories for the animals. I could read one for you, if you —"

"Yes! Read me one!"

Gaby felt warm all over. Her mom always had this effect on her. When her mom was home, just waking up in the morning earned Gaby a hundred little kisses. Getting an A on a test called for a full five-minute "happy dance," which was really a funkier version of the chicken dance. Gaby opened the notebook to Bonita's profile, a young Chinese shar-pei that Dr. Villalobos had trained to shake hands and roll over.

BONITA

My name is Spanish for pretty, but I'm a
Chinese shar-pei. I have a lot of folds and loose
wrinkles, but that doesn't mean I'm old and
ready to retire. I'm an energetic four-month-old
ball of tan-and-white fluff that needs exercise
every day. Wait till you see the tricks I've
learned at Furry Friends. Do you want me to
sit and stay? I can do that! Shake hands? I
can do that, too! Woof woof! That's Chinese
shar-pei for visit Furry Friends Animal Shelter
and take me home today!

Gaby backed away from the phone receiver. She knew
what was coming.

"Ooooooh, Gaby! I love it!" her mom screamed. "I love
it soooooooo much!"

"See? If you hurry up and come home, you could help
me with the animals at the shelter," Gaby said. "There's this
cat named Feather. She is so beautiful. You'd love her. We
could adopt her."

"I'm sure I would love her . . ." Her voice trailed off. "I better say good-bye. I know Mr. Gomez and Alma will be there soon to take you to school. Have a good day, *prin* —"

"Mom, you haven't changed your mind or anything, have you? You're still coming home, right?"

Her mom was silent for a few seconds.

"Mom?"

"Yes, Gaby," her mom finally said. "I promise."

Chapter 9

Before her class headed to the shelter, Gaby found herself unable to take her eyes off the map of the world that hung on the wall in the library. The map was new. Gaby would know, because she visited the library several times a day. She didn't have a computer at home like most of the girls, so she used the library's computers to do homework and write e-mails to her mom.

She zoned in on Honduras. Nestled between Nicaragua and Guatemala, the small country was shaded in purple, one of Gaby's favorite colors. She located San Pedro Sula on the map. Her mom's route would start there. She traced a path with her finger from San Pedro Sula through Guatemala. Her mom rarely spoke about her first journey to the United States, but a few times she had mentioned a train that coursed through Central America. Many migrants, like her, rode it to get to the United States. Then her mom would close her eyes, cover her face with her hands, and shake her head slowly. Her mom was only six years older than Gaby when she made the trip to the United States. Gaby shivered. She couldn't imagine traveling alone across desserts, mountains, and rivers. Whenever her mom recalled something bad about that journey, Gaby threw her arms around her mom's neck and hugged her for a long time. Gaby called this the "eraser hug." One full embrace and everything that hurt would disappear. Only happiness remained. It always worked on her mom, who after a few minutes would smile and tell Gaby that the journey was worth it and she'd do it again if she had to, because "you are here." Now, Gaby was counting on that.

She continued to trace a path through Mexico, where she passed over states with names that seemed to use every letter in the alphabet and took her entire mouth to pronounce. Gaby was practicing Tapachula, Oaxaca, Zacatecas, and Chihuahua out loud when she was nudged by Dolores.

"Let me guess, you're trying to figure out a way to break the rest of your family into the States?" said Dolores. She put her arm around Gaby's shoulders like they were pals.

Dolores was not her pal by any means. Gaby pulled out from under Dolores's arm. When she did, she bumped into Jan and dropped her notebook full of profiles. Before Gaby could grab it, Dolores scooped it up and started flipping through the pages.

"Give it back, Dolores," Gaby demanded.

"Make me," she said. The two eighth graders hovered over the notebook and giggled. "What are these little animal stories and sketches?"

Gaby felt her face flush.

"Probably for their service project at the animal shelter." Jan snickered. "I heard they have to clean up dog poop. So disgusting."

"She's probably good at that kind of work." Dolores smirked. "Your mom cleaned toilets, right?"

The comment stung Gaby. Sure, her mom cleaned toilets if that's what the job called for. Her mom was a hard worker. She cleaned homes and watched after babies so those babies' parents could work. She also did ten-hour shifts at the dry-cleaning factory. No one had the right to talk about her mom that way.

"Give it back, Dolores." Gaby lunged forward and

grabbed at the notebook, but for a skinny girl, Dolores's grip was tight.

"These are hilarious! Check this one out. 'My name is Feather. I was left at a rest stop by my owners, who no longer loved me.'" Dolores's head fell back as she burst into a fit of laughter. "That is so pathetic!"

Gaby glanced over at the desk where Sister Wendy, who ran the library, usually sat, but she wasn't there. Dolores laughed like a hyena, and her whole body shook. Gaby fought back the urge to tackle Dolores right there in the library. Instead, she made one more swipe for her notebook, finally freeing it. She turned to run, but instead slammed headfirst onto the carpeted floor. Jan had tripped her.

"Jan Nicole!" Sister Joan roared. "Get over here right now. You, too, Dolores Marie!"

Gaby looked up from the floor at Sister Wendy and Sister Joan standing in the library entrance. Sister Joan's face was as red as a tomato. Sister Wendy walked over and helped Gaby gather her notebook and papers into her book bag. Once up on her feet, Gaby felt her throat tighten and tears form in her eyes. Sister Wendy put her arm around Gaby's shoulder like a warm shawl. In a soft voice she told her, "Don't cry, sweetie. Don't give them the pleasure."

Gaby took a deep breath. Even though tears rimmed her eyes, she wasn't going to let Dolores and Jan see her cry.

Sister Joan grabbed Dolores and Jan by the elbows. "You two are coming with me!"

Gaby could hear their sniffling and phony excuses as they walked down the hallway to Sister Joan's office.

"Are you alright, Gaby?" Sister Wendy asked once they were gone.

Gaby nodded. "I think so." She took a deep breath. "Can I go now?"

"Of course, dear."

Gaby darted down the hallway toward the waiting bus parked in front of the school. She was relieved to find Alma waiting for her outside. It was time to go to the shelter.

"Where've you been, *chica*?" Alma asked.

"Dolores took my notebook."

"She what?!" Alma charged toward the school.

Gaby grabbed Alma's sweater and pulled her back like a fisherman reeling in a swordfish. "It's okay. I've got it now." She guided Alma to a seat on the bus.

"Standing there looking at Dolores and Jan, I realized something frightening."

"What?"

"They are dumber than we thought."

"Sweet St. Ann! How is that possible?" Alma exclaimed. "What did they say to you? Are you okay?"

"I'm fine." Gaby shrugged, but it was a lie. She couldn't

get Dolores's ugly words out of her head. It wasn't that Dolores read Feather's profile and called it "pathetic." It was what Dolores said about her mom. It wasn't the first time she'd heard Dolores talk that way, but it was the first time Gaby ever felt like she could smack her in the face. Her mom was beautiful and kind. Hardworking and generous. No one was going to call her names. As the bus pulled away from the school, Gaby closed her eyes and gave herself an eraser hug.

chapter 10

From outside, the coffee shop looked intimidating, with its patio and large windows revealing leather couches and a fireplace inside. Even the name, Café le Bean, made Gaby feel like she and Alma shouldn't enter. Now, she regretted raising her hand when Daisy asked for volunteers. At the time, she thought hanging up flyers at nearby shops would help her to forget the run-in with Dolores and Jan, but these were the types of businesses where people like her mom mopped the floor and people like Dolores's mom chugged coffee.

Gaby now wished she had stayed at the shelter and found a way to spend time with Feather.

"Alma, maybe Mrs. Kohler should come in with us." Gaby grabbed Alma's arm to stop her from entering the coffee shop. "They probably don't want kids in there."

"Remember, we come in the name of Furry Friends." Alma pushed her shoulders back and held her head high. "And we won't leave until they let us post a flyer . . . or two. Even if we have to chain ourselves to the cappuccino machine, we won't leave." Alma opened the door and headed straight to the counter. It was the first time Gaby had been inside a coffee shop.

She nudged Alma with her elbow. "What smells so good?"

"It's our coffee bean of the day!" said the girl at the counter with a black Café le Bean apron. "It's from Ethiopia." The girl's name tag said "Barista Chloe."

"Hi, Barista Chloe, may I speak with your manager?" asked Alma.

Gaby's eyes wandered toward a covered glass counter full of pastries. She wasn't a fan of sugary sweets, but these pastries were different. There were fruit Danishes drizzled with icing, thick slices of breads, large double chocolate chip cookies, and something called scones. Gaby dipped her hands into her pockets to find the five dollars her father gave her. She pulled it out and then saw a woman across the café cleaning tables. The woman's long black hair was pulled into a tight ponytail. She wore a crisp white apron over jeans and a black shirt. No special name tag. She looked up at Gaby, smiled for a second, and went back to wiping tables. Gaby unfolded the five-dollar bill.

"We would like to post a flyer for the Furry Friends Animal Shelter here." Alma spread out the flyers on the counter. "There are dozens of cats and dogs who need a safe, loving home." She handed Chloe the flyer for Pouncer. "Like this one."

POUNCER

I'm a yellow shorthaired female kitten with three months of life experience in smiles, giggles, and severe cuteness. Pouncer is my name and stalking is my game! I like to jump on anything that moves — even your feet! So wear your slippers around me! Is that a fly I see buzzing around you? Have no fear! I love to pounce and swat. I will take care of that little winged beast in ten seconds. Visit me at Furry Friends Animal Shelter and take me home today!

Chloe covered her mouth with her hand. "Who wrote this?" She looked like she was going to cry. Gaby backed up toward the door in case she needed to make a quick escape.

"Gaby wrote it." Alma gestured for Gaby to step up to the counter. She hesitantly approached. "We volunteer at the shelter."

"You're a good writer!"

"Thanks." Gaby smiled.

"I'm sure my boss won't mind posting these. I'll get him." Chloe walked to the back of the store and returned with a man wearing the same black Café le Bean apron. His name tag said "Master Barista Joel."

"Hi, girls, what can I do for you?"

Alma laid a flyer in front of him. "We'd like to post a flyer for Furry Friends Animal Shelter —"

The man shook his head. "Can't do it, sorry." He pushed the flyer back toward Alma.

"My teacher, Mrs. Kohler, is outside in the car. Would you like to talk to her?" She slid the flyer back across the counter to him.

He shook his head again. "That won't be necessary. Look, if I let you post a flyer, I'll have to let everyone post flyers," he said. "We're simply not that kind of place."

"This is not the kind of place that cares about homeless dogs and cats?" Alma spread out flyers for Bonita, Puck,

Secret, Cinder, Coco, and Lemon. Chloe frowned. Gaby pressed her money back into her front pocket and looked over at the woman cleaning tables.

"I respect your opinion, sir, but I think your patrons would disagree," Alma said. She reached out for Gaby's arm and pulled her closer. "Gaby and I volunteer at the shelter. One thing we've learned is how much this community values and supports local businesses and the local animal shelter. I bet you even have some patrons who have adopted dogs or cats from there." Earlier, Alma used the same argument on the hair salon owner down the street. The salon now had flyers on the front window and near the bathrooms.

The manager scratched the back of his head. Gaby and Chloe gazed at him with pleading eyes. Alma held out Cinder's flyer. "Please read it," she said. "You will see that these are not ordinary flyers. Ours tell stories written by a future award-winning writer." She winked slyly at Gaby. "If you don't like it, we'll go back to the shelter and never bother you again."

He took the flyer.

"Be ready to chain yourself to the cappuccino machine," Alma whispered to Gaby.

The flyer had a photo of shy Cinder with a Frisbee in her mouth and a short description written by Gaby. She had spent an entire afternoon writing and revising Cinder's profile. It had to be perfect because if anyone deserved a good home, it was Cinder. As the man read, Gaby watched his face.

CINDER

My name is Cinder and I am a one-year-old female rottweiler. Before I came to the Furry Friends Animal Shelter, I lived my life on a chain. I spent most of my days sad, hoping someone would play with me or show me some kindness. I'm missing a piece of my ear and tail, but I can still listen when you want to talk and I can still wag my tail whenever you are near. I am shy about meeting new people, but once I get to know and trust you, I will be your most loyal friend. Please visit me at Furry Friends Animal Shelter and take me home!

The master barista looked up at Alma. "Do you need tape?"

"Thank you so much!" Alma gushed, giving him and Chloe a high five. Gaby could hardly believe it. Her profile had changed his mind. While Alma and Chloe excitedly rushed over to the café entrance to post the flyers, Gaby pulled the money out of her pocket. She wanted to celebrate with a special treat. She gazed over the counter full of baked goods and her mouth watered, but then she thought about the woman cleaning tables. Maybe she had children at home. Maybe this was her second or third job.

Gaby approached her and held out the money. *"Para usted y su familia."*

The woman put her rag down. *"No, señorita."* The woman smiled and held her hands up to refuse the money. *"No gracias."*

"Please — *por favor* — if my mom were here she'd want you to have it," Gaby said, pushing the money toward her. "It's not much, I know . . ."

The woman looked closer at Gaby, as if trying to figure out if she knew her from somewhere. "I know your mom? What's her name?"

"Paloma Ramirez." The woman nodded in recognition and Gaby's whole body lifted. "What's your name?"

"Carolina." The woman smiled and then folded her

hands around Gaby's, closing the money inside. "You keep your money, *señorita*. Buy something for you and your friend." She glanced toward the counter. "The scones are really good. I make them this morning."

Gaby looked down at the five dollars in her hand. "I've never had a scone before." She shrugged. "This is my first time in a fancy café."

Carolina leaned in closer. "Maybe, next time you bring your mom and we can have coffee and scones together."

"I'd like that," Gaby smiled. *"Gracias."*

Gaby joined Alma at the counter.

"Do you know that woman?" Alma asked.

"I do now. She makes the scones." Gaby bought an orange frosted scone and shared it with Alma. As they headed out of the café, Carolina waved to them. "She was right," Gaby said. "The scones are good." The girls waved back and headed to the next business.

Chapter 11

The next week at the shelter, Dr. Villalobos was in the middle of his story about Lulu, a Labradoodle that had been adopted two days after she was brought into the shelter, when a fire truck pulled into the shelter's parking lot. From the front window, Gaby watched it park.

"Everyone wanted that dog," Dr. V. chuckled. "I thought I'd have to fight folks off with this broom." He grabbed a broom from against the wall and raised it like a sword and lunged.

"Um . . . we have visitors." Gaby pointed toward the parking lot.

All of the girls ran to the front door and watched three firemen in gray sweat suits jump out of the truck. Gaby smoothed her hair down.

Alma made her way through the girls to the front door.

"Let's go see what's smoking," she said. Gaby and all of the girls followed her outside in one big, giggling, huddled mass. "Where's the fire?" Alma yelled.

All the girls swooned when the tallest one stepped forward and ran his hand over his cropped, dark hair. "No fire, we're here to see about a dog," he said. He pulled a flyer out of his pocket and handed it to Alma. All the girls gasped as if he had dropped down on one knee and proposed to Alma right there on the spot. The girls quickly named him "Hottie."

"Hey, they're looking for Cinder!" Alma waved the flyer over her head. "C'mon, we'll show her to you." She took the fireman by the hand and led him to the backyard cages where Cinder stayed.

Gaby rushed to open Cinder's pen, but right away realized her mistake. The three men approached and Cinder retreated to the corner. "It's okay, sweetie." Cinder covered her muzzle with her paws and whimpered. Gaby squatted and gestured to the firemen to do the same. "These guys are good guys. They want to meet you. C'mon, shy girl."

The firemen looked at one another and frowned. Soon all the girls were calling for Cinder, but the young rottweiler wasn't budging. The more they called for her, the more she curled into a ball. A big rottweiler ball. Gaby bit down on her bottom lip. She had to do something.

"Maybe she isn't ready to come home with us," said the fireman with the gray hair and light blue eyes. Behind his back, the girls nicknamed him "Smokey."

His words alarmed Gaby. Of course Cinder was ready. All of the dogs were ready for a home. The girls looked back and forth at one another, desperate for ideas.

"Alma, go grab a Frisbee," Gaby said.

"You're a genius!" Alma shouted as she ran off. Her classmates shook their heads as if they were thinking, "This is not the time to be playing." Gaby shrugged. It was worth a try. Soon a neon orange disc sailed over their heads. Hottie caught it.

Everyone spread out. He sent it flying back to Alma.

Just as Gaby had hoped, Cinder shot up. On all fours now, she watched the Frisbee fly past her with steady eyes. Gaby knew Cinder couldn't resist a good game of Frisbee. Alma snapped it to the fireman that all the girls thought looked like Zac Efron's twin. They nicknamed him "Sizzler."

Cinder took a few steps. Sizzler threw the Frisbee to Gaby.

"Ready, Cinder?" Gaby shouted. Cinder squatted low and set her eyes on the orange disc. Gaby threw it. Cinder ran and jumped for it, catching it in her mouth. Everyone cheered. She galloped around before she dropped it at Gaby's feet. The firemen knelt next to Cinder. Now, it was their time for nicknaming. They stroked her back and called her "pretty girl" and "sweetie pie." Cinder wagged her tail and opened her mouth wide into a big goofy smile. Sizzler took Cinder's torn ear into his hands. He winced as he examined it. The girls quieted.

"Cinder was abused, but she's healthy now and very sweet," Gaby said.

"She's a survivor," he said. Cinder licked him and he took her face between his hands and kissed her back. "Sounds like she's perfect for us."

Gaby was so happy she felt like giving him a big kiss, but of course she didn't. Cinder was now kissing him enough for the both of them.

After completing their adoption paperwork, the firemen walked back to their truck with Cinder on a leash. Dr. Villalobos shook the firemen's hands and then got down on his knees and whispered into Cinder's ear, followed by a big hug.

"Get a room!" Alma heckled him.

The firemen were about to put Cinder into the truck, when Gaby yelled for them to wait. She rushed up to Hottie.

"You promise never to chain her up?" she asked.

"She'll never be chained again. At the station, she'll be

free to roam," he said. "We're going to play Frisbee every day, and Cinder will eat steak with us."

Gaby handed him Cinder's flyer. "I signed this for you."

"Thanks. I'll frame it at the station."

As the truck pulled away with Cinder, the girls shouted farewells and blew kisses. Then it happened. Cinder stuck her head out the window and looked back at the girls. She opened her mouth wide and let her tongue roll out. All the girls pointed and squealed. For Cinder, the feeling of the wind against her face must have been as great as the first time the young pup felt the chain unclasp from her neck. She was free. She was safe. And she had a home.

Chapter 12

Once the fire truck was gone, Mrs. Kohler called for the girls to get back to cleaning. The girls groaned. Gaby dreaded cleaning the dog cages, but it was a messy job made easier by Dr. Villalobos's presence. He always tagged along and shared stories about the dogs in the shelter, which gave Gaby fresh material for her profiles. She and Alma turned to head back to the dog room when a silver BMW approached.

"OMG. That is my dad's dream car," Alma said.

"Maybe they're here to adopt," Gaby said.

"Hope so!"

"What if they want to adopt Spike? You won't be sad?"

"Nah, he's a crazy mutt. All my work converting him into a sane dog is so that he'll find a home. If someone actually adopted him, I'd be like '*Adios*, crazy dog!' "

Gaby shook her head. She wasn't buying any of that. She'd seen the way Alma looked at Spike with tenderness and the way Spike followed her around the shelter. The whole time Gaby had been occupied with writing profiles, Alma had been falling in love with a crazy terrier that thought "stay" meant to take off like a rocket. Gaby knew he'd already taken off with Alma's heart.

"Oh well, back to work!" Alma threw up her hands and walked away.

Gaby stopped and stayed. Dr. V. was still outside at the entrance watching the silver car park. A man and woman hopped out of the car and strutted up the sidewalk like supermodels. Dr. Villalobos didn't budge, which Gaby thought was strange. He was usually so excited about any guest to the shelter. This time, he just stared down at his shoes and waited.

From the front desk, Daisy called Gaby to help fold newsletters. The task was tedious, but better than cleaning cages, so Gaby jumped on it. Soon, the couple and Dr. V.

passed the front desk. "Like I told you on the phone, she is still in the clinic recovering, but I have no problem showing her to you," Dr. V. said. "It's the only way to know if she truly is your cat."

Gaby froze midfold. Did she just hear what she thought she heard? Could it be true?

"Something wrong with the newsletters?" Daisy asked.

"No, no. It's fine," Gaby said. "I think those people were Feather's owners."

Daisy rushed to the edge of the desk to catch a glimpse, but they'd already passed. "I wondered if they'd show up," she said.

"What do you mean?"

"They called and said they'd lost their cat. They e-mailed a photo and everything. It was Feather. Then they never showed up and we didn't hear from them again." She shook her head. "Doesn't seem to me like they're entirely committed to getting their pet back, which I can't understand. Feather is a beautiful cat."

"Aren't they the ones that left her at a rest stop?"

"They said she jumped out of the car when they stopped and they couldn't find her," Daisy said. "They had to leave her behind. Anyway, that's their story."

Gaby chewed on her bottom lip. Surely Dr. V. wouldn't release her to them. Would he?

"Oh shoot!" Gaby exclaimed. "I left something in the dog room. I got to go. Sorry!"

"Do what you got to do, kiddo."

Gaby ran to the clinic. The door was cracked open. She peeked inside and saw the woman and man in front of the cages. Dr. V. wasn't there. As the man opened a cage and pulled out Feather, Gaby was ready to barge in and tell him to stop when the woman spoke.

"Poor Malbec," she said. The man handed Feather to her.

They were Feather's owners. Gaby moved closer. Malbec? What kind of name was that?

Feather hung her head over the woman's arm. Gaby knew she was no expert in animal behavior, but Feather didn't seem happy to be found.

The guy shrugged. "Have you forgotten that you did nothing but complain about that dumb fur ball's hair on your clothes?"

Gaby gasped. How dare he call Feather a dumb fur ball! Suddenly, Dr. V. was at Gaby's side.

"Anything interesting?"

She jumped. "Sorry, it's — I didn't want to interrupt — they're talking."

"Not to worry. Come on in." Dr. V. chuckled and pushed the clinic door open. "I have some files I need you to take to

Daisy." She followed him inside. "Sorry for the wait, folks. I'll be right with you."

While Dr. V. flipped through files, Gaby smiled at the couple. Feather mewed and stretched a paw toward Gaby.

"Stop it." The woman shoved Feather's paw down.

Dr. V. slammed the file cabinet drawer. "Feather's been through a lot. Please be gentle with her." The woman nodded with an annoyed, thin smile.

"Her name is Malbec," the man said. "Feather sounds like something a bunch of little girls would come up with."

Dr. Villalobos ignored the comment and faced Gaby. "Here you go, sweetheart." He handed her a file. "Please take this to Daisy."

Before leaving, Gaby stopped and turned back to the couple. "What does Malbec mean?"

"I'm sorry?" The man's eyebrows rose like he was surprised Gaby could speak.

"You called her Malbec."

"Oh, it's a French wine," the woman explained.

"It's Argentinean. Not French. I've told you a million times," the man said.

Dr. V. and Gaby exchanged bewildered looks.

"Just wondering." Gaby smiled. "I'm glad you found your cat." The man looked at his watch and the woman looked down at Feather as if she'd forgotten she was even holding a cat. "Missed her like crazy, I bet." Gaby winked and walked out.

When Gaby got back to the front desk, Daisy wasn't there. She sat down and resumed folding newsletters. Her head was still reeling from that snooty-snotty couple. The man had looked at her like, "How dare she speak to me!" And Malbec? What kind of name was that for a sweet cat? Flustered by the encounter, she dropped a bunch of newsletters onto the floor. She had bent over to pick them up when she heard the couple's agitated voices coming down the hallway. When they stopped at the front entrance, Gaby stayed down. One run-in with them was enough.

"I say, let him keep her. She's so sick and scrawny looking," said the man.

Gaby's mouth gaped open. If Feather looked sick and scrawny it was because they left her at a rest stop to starve. She was tempted to hurl the stapler at him, but restrained herself.

"Don't exaggerate," the woman said. She threw her hands up. "I don't care about his stupid waiting list. We're lawyers, for god's sake! We can sue him if he refuses to give Malbec back to us."

They exited the shelter. Gaby sat up and watched them drive away in their shiny silver car. She may not know about fancy French and Argentinean wines, but Gaby knew one thing for sure: That couple didn't deserve to have Feather.

ChaPTeR 13

Later that afternoon, Gaby spread out notes on her front porch. She passed a page to Alma. "It says we have to show that we are the alpha dog. What does that mean?" After the girls returned from the shelter, they had gone to the library to do research. While Alma printed dog training tips, Gaby read up on Furry Friends Animal Shelter's adoption policy. She was disappointed to discover that there wasn't a policy against calling a cat a dumb fur ball. If she could rewrite the policy, she'd add in big bold print that anyone who leaves their cat or dog at a rest stop should not even bother coming to Furry Friends.

"We have to show them who the boss is," Alma explained. "Not mean. Stern. You know, like our moms and dads are with us —" Alma stopped, but it was too late.

Gaby turned away. "I wouldn't know about that."

Alma stared down at the notes as if an answer was buried in between the tips on how to teach a dog to roll over, sit, and stay. "What do you mean you don't know?" she finally managed to say. "Your dad may not be exactly parent material, but your mom used to be very stern with us. Remember how all of us used to fight? Your mom would walk into the room and be like 'Alma Victoria Gomez!' or 'Marcos Lorenzo Beltrán!'" Alma did her best Spanish accent and pointed with her finger.

Gaby smiled for a second. Her mom was tiny, but her voice was mighty. In English or in Spanish she knew how to get people's attention. If her mom had been given the opportunity to get an education, Gaby thought she would have made a great school principal.

"All your mom had to do was say our full names a certain way and we were angels," Alma continued. "You can't take care of crazy kids without being like an alpha dog."

"Especially if Marcos is one of those kids," Gaby added.

"Exactly!" Alma smiled, looking relieved that Gaby made a joke.

"Did someone say my name?" Marcos wheeled up and parked his bike against the fence. Enrique followed close behind. They had on soccer shorts and white Mexico national team jerseys smudged with grass stains.

"Let me guess — the grass won 4–0," Alma said.

Marcos rolled his eyes. Enrique wedged himself between Alma and Gaby.

"Don't I smell good?"

Gaby pinched her nose and quickly gathered up the notes.

Enrique grabbed at the pages. "Can I see?"

"No. It's none of your business." Gaby batted his hands away and passed all the papers to Alma.

"Why so secretive?" Enrique snatched at the notes again, but this time Alma slapped his hands down.

Gaby mouthed, "Be the alpha."

Alma nodded and sat up on her knees to make herself taller than Enrique, which was a major feat because no one was taller than Enrique. In a few more years, Gaby imagined, he'd be as tall as Dr. Villalobos. Alma clutched the papers close to her chest. Enrique lunged for them.

"Enrique Andrés García! Down!" she warned.

Enrique backed away. He looked over at Marcos for help. Marcos shrugged.

Alma was known for tussling with Enrique, screaming at him, and causing a wild scene that ended with someone, usually Enrique, being chased around the yard. He wasn't used to *this* Alma. He sat up, folded his arms across his chest, and pouted.

"What's the dealio? Why can't I see your love letters?" Again, he lunged for the notes.

"No, Enrique! Back!" Alma pointed at him and held the notes behind her back with the other hand. "Sit and stay."

Gaby now wished Alma could have met Feather's owners. She was certain that Alma would have stormed into the clinic, snatched Feather from the woman's arms, and chased them out of the shelter. Gaby chuckled.

After a few seconds, Enrique gave up. Alma shuffled the notes, watching him out of the corner of her eye. Enrique fidgeted with his shirt, his long socks, and his cleats, but kept his distance. Gaby shook her head in disbelief. Alma was a natural alpha dog at the shelter *and* in the neighborhood.

"Good boy, Enrique!" Alma exclaimed. "Gaby, do we have a treat we can give him?"

"I think I have a dog biscuit in my —"

"Hey, that's not right!" he wailed. "I prefer doggie bones." Everybody laughed.

"Since you're being so good, I'll show you the notes." Alma spread the pages out again. Enrique moved closer while she pointed out a few instructions on rewarding pets for good behavior. "This is what I do at the shelter."

"What's the point? You guys are only going to be there for a few more weeks, right? My Uncle Joe-Joe says dogs forget everything." He tugged at his socks.

"Maybe your Uncles Joe-Joe, Junior, and John-John don't know everything," Alma snapped. "The point is that the dogs have to be ready for our Barkapalooza open house. This way people will see how well trained they are and adopt them."

"How's that sick cat? Is she kaput yet?" Marcos asked. Both girls responded with a glare. "What? What did I say?"

"That sick cat's name is Feather and no, she's not kaput," Gaby said. "In fact, her owners showed up today. They want her back."

"That's good, isn't it?" Marcos asked.

"It'd be great if they weren't self-absorbed jerks," Gaby said.

"Whoa! Tell us how you really feel," Marcos quipped.

"Don't hold back, Gaby!" Enrique clapped.

"Gaby overheard them talking about how they might sue the shelter if Dr. V. doesn't release Feather to them," Alma said.

"They don't deserve Feather," Gaby said. "The man called her a dumb fur ball."

"We have to tell Dr. V.," said Alma. "If we tell him what you heard he won't give her back to them."

"But if Feather is their cat, they have the right to take her home," Enrique said.

"Not if they're unfit," Gaby added. "I wish my mom were here. We could adopt her, you know?"

"Don't worry, Gaby." Alma put her arms around Gaby's shoulder. "We'll talk to Dr. V."

Gaby felt tears well up in her eyes. If only she had enough money. If only her mom were here. She could ask her dad, but she knew what he'd say. He'd rant about how they barely have enough money to cover their bills. There was no money for a cat. She was pretty sure the City Harvest Center didn't hand out cat food.

The wind rustled the big tree in front of her house. Gaby watched the branches sway. If Feather was stuck in that tree — no matter how high she was — Gaby was certain she could save her. But this was different — and she felt helpless.

CHAPTER 14

It had been a week since they were last at the shelter. Even though Gaby and Alma had sent Dr. V. an e-mail about Feather's owners, Gaby was nervous that Dr. V. would be forced to release Feather to them. As soon as the bus parked, she ran to the clinic to see Feather.

"As far as I know the owners still want her," said Daisy. She took Feather out of her cage and passed her to Gaby. "But they haven't come back."

Gaby held Feather close and gazed into her perfect emerald eyes. "I hope they never do."

Daisy ruffled Gaby's hair. "C'mon, we've got lots of pictures to take today for our website."

The girls were split into two groups. With Daisy's help, one team took cat pictures inside. Dr. Villalobos, Mrs. Kohler, Alma, and Gaby were part of a second team to snap photos of the dogs outside. As the dogs were brought out of the shelter one by one, Gaby's job was to brush them to ensure they looked picture-perfect. Despite Atticus trying to eat the brush and Puck trotting up to the camera to give it a good slobbery lick, the photo session ran smoothly until Spike charged out of his cage like a bull.

Gaby rushed to catch him, but when he saw a toy bone lying in the grass, he clamped it between his teeth and ran off.

"Stop him!" Gaby screamed. The girls scampered around the lawn. Two girls tried to trap him by the oak tree, but just as they made a dive to the left, he swerved right and scurried off with the bone still in his mouth. The girls tumbled onto the grass.

Spike skidded to a stop by the fence at the farthest edge of the shelter's backyard. He sank to the grass and gnawed on the bone like it was a slab of barbeque ribs. Alma moved in with the camera.

"Now this will be a great picture," she said. "Sweet little Spike, my sweet little Spikey." His ears perked up as he watched Alma creep closer. Suddenly he barked, sprang up, and raced to the opposite side of the lawn where Gaby was ready . . . or so she thought.

As one girl lunged for him, Spike sped past and veered toward Gaby. All she saw was a blur of black and white. She squatted and dived.

"I got him!" Gaby rolled onto her back with Spike in her arms. He dropped the bone and smothered her face with licks until she didn't think she could breathe. Alma rushed over, snapped a quick picture, and whisked him away.

"Gaby, the dog tackler!" Dr. Villalobos held out his hand and helped her to her feet. Snowflake, an older white cat, was draped around his neck.

"Nice scarf, Dr. V.," she quipped.

Dr. V. chuckled and stroked Snowflake's tail. Even though Snowflake had free-roaming rights, which meant she didn't need a cage because she had the whole shelter, she preferred to sit atop people's shoulders and wrap herself around their necks. In the shelter world, "free-roaming" was the highest honor and reserved for only the best-behaved cats or dogs. It was an honor, Gaby was sure, that crazy Spike would never enjoy. She brushed grass from her sweater and pants.

"Any word from Feather's owners?"

"I just got off the phone with them, actually." Dr. V.

frowned. Gaby's heart stopped. "They say they'll come for Feather tomorrow. And if I don't hand her over, they'll file a lawsuit." Across the yard, a girl yelled for Dr. V. "I'll be right there, Rachel," he said. "I'm sorry, Gaby." He started to walk away.

"Let them sue!" Gaby hollered behind him. He turned back to her. "I'll tell the judge what I heard them say," Gaby said. "I'm not afraid."

"They work for one of the biggest law firms in town."

"But the shelter reserves the right to refuse. It says so on the website."

"Believe me, Gaby. I wouldn't turn Feather over to them if I didn't think they could win. Even if they didn't win . . . going to court isn't cheap. The shelter would suffer. You did the right thing in telling me everything you heard. Don't forget that." He walked away.

Gaby bit down on her lip. She looked around the yard. Daisy was inside helping some girls with the cat photos. Everyone else, including Dr. Villalobos and Mrs. Kohler, was outside.

"Why so serious?" Alma was suddenly in front of her holding Spike.

"My book bag . . . I need it . . . It's in the office," Gaby stammered. "I had an idea for Spike's profile. I need my notebook." She marched past Alma.

Alma shouted behind her, "You go, girl! I can't wait to read it!"

Gaby hated lying to Alma, but she had to do something. Like her mom had told her over and over, *"Animales* depend on us to take care of them." If she was going to save Feather, now was her chance.

ChAPTeR 15

After grabbing her book bag from the office, Gaby poked her head into the clinic.

"Hello?" She crept in and closed the door behind her.

Through the walls, Gaby could hear voices from the cat room. The girls were telling the cats to "smile for the camera." Good luck with that, Gaby thought. She found a towel on the counter, stuffed it into her book bag, and tiptoed to the cages. Feather was asleep. "It's okay, sweet Feather," Gaby whispered. "I'm here to save you."

Gaby unlatched Feather's cage. Suddenly the cat from the cage below Feather's reached out and snagged her. "My sweater!" Gaby gasped. Most days, she left her sweater on the bus, as all the girls did, but today she had been in too much of a rush to see Feather and had forgotten. As Gaby stepped back, the cat's claws tightened on her sweater, ripping out strands of dark blue threads. The cat wailed. Its claws were tangled. "No, don't cry, kitty. It's okay."

Gaby looked back toward the door and hoped no one came in to see what all the noise was about. After some tugging, she freed the cat's claws from her sweater, but the damage was done. Her only good sweater was wrecked. Worse, the poor cat was nursing its paw.

"I'm so sorry," Gaby said softly. On the floor was an opened sack of dry cat food. She scooped some out and passed it to the cat. "There you go. This will make it all better." The cat stopped licking its paw and ate the food.

Gaby reached into Feather's cage and took gentle hold of her by the back of the neck. Feather's green eyes opened slightly and then closed. She was grateful that Feather was napping. She lowered Feather into her book bag and zipped it, leaving a slight opening for air to get through. She stuffed both her pockets with dry cat food until they bulged. Gaby strapped the book bag on her back and had her hand on the doorknob ready to leave when she realized Mrs. Kohler was on the other side of the door calling for the girls to gather their things.

Gaby put her ear against the clinic door and waited. She could go out the other door, but that led outside. She didn't want to risk anyone seeing her leave the clinic. Finally, Mrs. Kohler's voice trailed off. Gaby opened the door just enough to peek. All was clear. She closed it behind her and joined the girls in the parking lot waiting to board the bus.

Alma waved her over. "Gaby, your sweater! What happened?"

Gaby winced and patted down the loose threads. "Yeah . . ." she stalled. "The craziest thing, it snagged on my notebook."

"The hazards of being a shelter scribe." Alma shrugged.

"Yeah, exactly." Gaby pulled tight on her book bag straps. She hoped Feather was still asleep. If this was going to work, she needed to keep Feather as quiet as possible. Alma would be the real challenge. If Gaby was hiding something, it would be a matter of seconds before Alma figured it out.

"Oh hey, I have to ask Carly something. I'll see you on the bus." She left Alma standing there, looking wounded.

On the bus, even though Alma had saved Gaby a window seat next to her, Gaby took the empty seat behind her. Again, Alma looked hurt. Gaby wished she could erase

Alma's pout, but she knew she couldn't involve her right now. Once she got Feather settled, safely away from the shelter, she'd tell her everything. She'd understand.

Gaby sat the book bag on her lap and peeked inside. Feather still slept.

"Everything there?" Alma kneeled backward on the seat in front of Gaby and smiled down at her. Gaby clutched the book bag shut.

"Alma, you know I don't want to see you sitting that way on the bus," Mrs. Kohler reminded her from the front of the bus. "Please take your proper seat."

Alma made a sour face and sat down. Just then, Feather meowed.

Gaby's heart stopped. All the girls giggled and looked around. Gaby put the book bag on the floor of the bus and dug into her pockets for cat food.

"Was that a cat?" a girl asked.

Feather cried out again. All the girls giggled and peeked under their seats. Gaby clutched the morsels of cat food in her hand. She had to find a way to quiet Feather.

"It was just me!" Gaby said nervously. A couple of girls crowded into the seat across the aisle from her.

"It sounded so real!" a girl said. "Do it again."

Gaby produced a soft, drawn-out meow. It sounded nothing like Feather.

"No, no, it was better the first time. Do it the way you did it before."

"Yeah, how did you do that?"

"Do it again."

Suddenly, there was a bark. All the girls exploded in laughter. It was Alma.

"What is going on back there?" Mrs. Kohler exclaimed.

"Woof! Woof!" Alma turned around and barked some more.

Soon all the girls were barking, howling, and meowing back at one another until the bus was as loud as the shelter. When Gaby thought no one was watching, she dipped her hand into the bag and fed Feather from her palm. She looked up. Alma was watching her. She glanced from the book bag to Gaby, shook her head slowly, and sat back down without a word.

ChAPTER 16

When the bus parked at St. Ann's, Gaby and Alma were the first off. The parking lot was empty. School had let out fifteen minutes ago. Alma's mother waved from her car. Gaby slid into the backseat, while Alma took the front.

"Hi, Mrs. Gomez," Gaby said. She pulled off her backpack and rested it on the floor.

"Hey, sweetheart! You girls got everything?"

"Yes," Gaby answered.

"And more," Alma added. Gaby froze. Was Alma going to tell on her? She wouldn't dare! Would she?

Gaby smiled at Alma through the passenger mirror, but Alma ignored her. If it wasn't for Alma, Gaby was sure that right now she'd be in Sister Joan's office, also known as the "dungeon," trying to explain how a cat got into her book bag. Gaby unzipped the bag to give Feather some air.

Suddenly, Feather's paw shot out from the bag and batted around as if it wanted to smack some sense into Gaby. It worked.

Gaby blinked. Was there really a cat — a full-grown cat — in her book bag? The evidence was there in the navy blue shreds of her sweater. Suddenly, she felt hot all over. She pulled off her torn cardigan. How was she going to take care of Feather? How was she going to keep her hidden from her father? How was she going to fix her sweater?

Feather was still reaching out of the bag, swiping at the air. Luckily, Alma's mom was singing along to a popular song. If Feather meowed, she wouldn't notice. Feather dropped her paw back down. The bag bulged east and west, north and south as Feather moved. After a few seconds, it seemed like the cat had finally settled down. Gaby relaxed against the backseat. Soon Feather popped her paw out again like she wanted a high five. Gaby giggled and tapped it. The paw sunk back down. After a few minutes it was back up. It was their game all the way home.

Since it was Friday, Gaby was staying at Alma's house. Friday was Gaby's favorite night of the week, because every Friday at Alma's house was Mexican-food-and-a-movie night. Alma's mom made the best enchiladas and Alma's father had a secret recipe for guacamole that she craved.

When they reached the house, the girls went straight up to Alma's room. Alma locked the bedroom door behind them.

"I cannot believe you smuggled that cat from the shelter, Gaby!" Alma was pacing the room. "That's just all kinds of wrong! What were you thinking?"

Gaby let Feather out of her book bag and onto her twin bed. Feather gazed around the room and pawed Gaby's pillow. Gaby sat on the edge of bed. "I had no choice."

Alma paused and raised an eyebrow. "No choice?" She shook her head. "Maybe I should have let you get busted on the bus. It's obvious our friendship means nothing to you."

Gaby looked up, shocked. "But that's not true. That's why I didn't tell you my plan. I didn't want you to get in trouble if Feather was discovered."

"No, instead you lied to me, Gaby. Best friends don't keep secrets or lie to each other." Alma folded her arms across her chest. "Especially if catnapping is involved."

Suddenly, there was a knock at the door. "Girls, what movie do you want Dad to pick up?" Alma's mom wiggled the doorknob. "Hey, why's the door locked?"

"What are we going to do?" Gaby whispered. She picked Feather up from the bed.

"I don't know . . ." Alma looked around wildly, then grabbed Feather from her and put the cat into the closet. It'd have to do for now.

Alma opened the door. "Hey, Mom! Sorry about that. What were you saying?"

Her mom looked around the room. "Everything okay?" She had already changed out of her work clothes and was wearing jeans and a sweatshirt.

Gaby watched the closet door. She hoped Feather wouldn't start meowing or scratching at it.

"Everything's fine. What were you saying about a movie?"

"Um, what movie do you want your dad to pick up?"

Alma tapped her lips with a single finger. "I'm thinking something like *Catwoman*, maybe? What do you think, Gaby? We've never seen that."

All Gaby could muster was a quick shake of her head.

"How about *The Cat in the Hat*?" Alma continued.

"Seen it already." Gaby narrowed her eyes at Alma. What was she doing?

"What's this sudden obsession with cats, Alma?" her mom asked.

"Maybe you should ask Gaby."

Gaby swallowed hard. "Cats are fascinating creatures . . . and we have a lot to learn from them. Like how to stretch properly and stuff. That's all."

"Okay, a cat movie it is." Her mom turned to leave, but stopped in the doorway. "I'll be making yummy enchiladas if you want to come down and help."

As soon as Alma shut the bedroom door, Gaby pulled Feather from the closet. She held her close to her chest. "Sorry, Feather. Was it dark inside there?"

"No, but it's dark in your book bag."

"Look, Alma. I couldn't let those awful people take her."

Alma looked long and hard at Gaby. "What did Dr. V. say?"

Gaby kissed Feather on her head. "He said there was nothing he could do."

"That doesn't sound like Dr. V." Alma shook her head.

"He said they threatened to sue him. He had no choice. I had no choice. I had to save her."

"Do you know what this means? After Mrs. Kohler finds out what you did, your Furry Friends days are over."

"How will she find out? Feather will stay with me," Gaby said. "Those people don't deserve her. They named her Malbec. That's crazy!"

"True . . ." Alma let the word stretch out. "Still, your dad is going to freak. He doesn't exactly like cats and dogs."

"I've already figured it out. I'll keep her hidden in the basement during the week, and on weekends we can keep her up here. Once my mom comes back, my dad will move out and everything will be good again. It will be my mom, Feather, and me."

"No way, José! If you want to keep Feather here, you have to tell my parents. I'm not going to lie or sneak around."

"They'll tell my dad or take Feather back to the shelter." Gaby was on the verge of tears. "Besides, it won't be long. My mom will be home in a month or so. She just has to get more money."

"She told you she's coming home in a month?"

"Of course! We talked the other day." Gaby bit down on her lip. That wasn't exactly the truth. The truth was she didn't know when her mom would have enough money to make the trip home. She didn't exactly have a set timeline.

"Are you sure she's coming back, Gaby? It's been three months already."

"Actually, it's been three months, two weeks, and four days." Gaby scowled.

Both girls were silent. Feather meowed. Gaby held her tighter.

"My mom is coming home," Gaby finally said. She grabbed her book bag and put Feather back inside. "Sorry, Feather. Just a little while longer."

"What are you doing?"

"I'm going home." Gaby wished she could stop the sneaking around, but it was too late now. It made her angry that Alma didn't back her up more.

"But it's Friday night, Gaby. You're supposed to be with us on weekends."

"I want to go home."

"This *is* your home on weekends."

"No. It's not. I'd rather move to Honduras than ever have this place be my home." Gaby grabbed her bag and walked out. Alma gasped.

"Gaby!" Alma yelled after her. Gaby stormed down the stairs and out the front door.

Chapter 17

At home, Gaby poured Feather a small bowl of milk, but Feather didn't touch it. She sat on the kitchen floor, looked around, and meowed. "You don't want milk? You want food?" Gaby put the leftover dry cat food from her pocket into a bowl. Feather twitched her nose at it. "Not hungry? What do you want?" Feather meowed some more. "A tour?"

Gaby picked up Feather and carried her to the refrigerator. "This is the fridge." She opened it and put the half gallon of milk back onto the top shelf. "It's kind of empty." An open carton with two eggs, half a loaf of bread, and bottles of ketchup and mustard sat on the second shelf.

Feather meowed and Gaby closed the refrigerator. She spun around and faced the sink. "Well, that's it for the kitchen. Not much, I know. When my mom was here, the kitchen always smelled great." She walked over to a cabinet and opened it. Piled on top of one another were mismatched ceramic plates. "My mom is from Honduras, so when she was here she always cooked fried plantains, empanadas, and tortillas with rice and beans." Feather nudged Gaby's face with her head as if saying, "Tell me more about those tortillas."

"My mom is in Honduras right now." Gaby kissed Feather's head. "Hopefully, she'll be home soon and you can try a homemade tortilla." Feather reached out and touched Gaby's face with her soft velvet paw and mewed. "Let's see the rest of the house."

Gaby opened the door to her father's room. It used to be her mom's room. Bedsheets were strewn everywhere. A mirror leaned against the wall. His shoes and belts were scattered on the floor. "My dad better clean this room before my mom gets back. She will *not* be happy." Gaby shook her head. "My dad is always looking for a new job because he says his bosses are nut jobs. He thinks cats are nut jobs, too, so you should avoid his room." Feather seemed to understand and produced a long shaky cry. "Don't worry. You're going to stay in the basement when I'm at school. I'll make a nice bed for you. You'll see. It'll be super cozy and it's only until my mom comes home."

She took Feather to her room. The walls were lavender. A folded comforter, sheet, and pillow sat on top of a mattress on the floor. "This is my room, but I don't sleep here anymore. One night, I had a dream that my mom was knocking on our door. She was trying to come back, but I didn't hear her knock, so she left."

Feather gave a gentle head butt to Gaby's chin.

"Lately, I have a lot of weird dreams like that. Always, my mom is knocking on our door. Now, I sleep on the couch so that when she comes back, I'll hear her."

Gaby grabbed a framed picture from the dresser. "That's me and my mom. Everyone says I look like her, which is good because she's pretty." The photo was from Gaby's ninth birthday. In the photo, her mom held a *tres leches* birthday cake decorated with candles. Gaby kissed the picture. "There are girls at school who call my mom illegal because my mom isn't a U.S. citizen." Feather rubbed her head against Gaby's neck. "But if they'd known her, they wouldn't call her names, because she loves everyone and everyone loves her."

Gaby put her mother's photo down and picked up another. "This is me and Alma. You met her earlier. She's the one that threw you in a closet." Feather pawed at it. "We've been best friends since first grade, but I guess that's all over." Gaby swallowed hard. "She can be impossible sometimes."

Feather gazed up at Gaby and meowed.

"You're right. I can be impossible, too."

In the living room, the only sign that her mom had ever lived there was the picture on the wall of all three of them. It was taken when her parents were still together. In the picture, her father seemed happy. His hair was slicked back with gel and he wore a blue shirt that matched his eyes. Gaby was in a yellow dress and sat on his lap. She'd never forget that day, because later that night she woke up crying. Back then, her father stayed home at night with her while her mom worked late. Gaby had cried because she had to go to the bathroom, but was too scared of the cockroaches that darted out of tight corners. Her father took her by the hand and walked her to the bathroom. As soon as he switched on the light, cockroaches scurried for cover. Gaby backed away and screamed.

"You're bigger than them, Gaby," he told her. "They're more scared of you."

The next day, her father fumigated the entire house and the roaches never came back. It was the last time she remembered holding her father's hand. It had felt warm and safe.

Maybe once upon a time he had wanted a daughter, but now he looked at Gaby like she was just another job he wanted to quit.

It was sort of like the cats at the shelter. Everyone wants the kittens, but no one wants the cats. And now that Gaby wasn't a kitten anymore, her father wasn't interested in hanging around.

She sighed. Besides that photo, there was nothing else about her mom to show Feather. The small vase of fresh-cut flowers her mom used to set at the center of the dining room table was now her father's penholder. The hardwood floor that her mom swept and polished every weekend was now dull. The reclining chair her mom bought at a garage sale and napped in after a long day at work remained unused.

She slumped down on the couch and grabbed the phone from the small table next to it. "Of all the things here, this phone is the most important," Gaby said. "Some girls sleep with teddy bears, but I sleep with the phone." Feather stared with both ears perked up. "I tuck it under my pillow so that if my mom calls, I'll hear it," she said. "I can't wait till I don't have to sleep with it anymore." Feather tilted her head like she understood every word.

"Look at us! We're both temporary strays, Feather!" She kissed Feather on the black M. "M for mom," she said.

Feather got up on her hind legs and rested her front paws and head on Gaby's shoulder. It was the cat version of the eraser hug.

"Thank you, Feather," Gaby said. "We might be strays, but we've got each other."

ChAPteR 18

Gaby hated putting Feather in the basement, but it was the safest place for her. If her father came home, he'd never go down there. She arranged newspaper on the floor, careful not to take her father's classified ads. She topped off a bowl with water and left an open can of tuna mixed with the left-over dry cat food she had taken. Gaby had barely finished making Feather's new bed, a laundry basket cushioned with an old blanket, when someone pounded on the front door. She hoped it was Alma.

"Coming!" Gaby yelled. More pounding. She took Feather with her and rushed upstairs. She looked out the peephole and growled. It wasn't Alma. It was Marcos.

She dropped Feather off in her bedroom. "I won't be long, Feather. It's only Marcos." Gaby brushed fur from her shirt, snatched her notebook from the couch, and opened the front door.

"Hey, what took you so long?" Marcos handed her a plastic container. "Cheese enchiladas from the Gomezes."

"*Gracias.*"

"*De nada,*" Marcos said. He looked past her and toward the inside of the house. "Aren't you going to invite me in?"

Gaby stepped onto the porch and shut the screen door behind her. "Why? It's so nice outside."

"Whatever." Marcos pulled his jacket's hood over his head and took a seat on the porch steps. He fiddled with his jacket zipper. "I was just at Alma's house. I figured you'd be there. It's Friday night, you know? What's up with that?"

"She knew you were coming to my house?"

"Duh! That's why they sent me with the enchiladas."

"Did she tell you anything?"

"About what?" Marcos shrugged. "Wait a minute! Are you and Alma mad at each other?" He shook his head. "What are you two fighting about? Not me, I hope."

Gaby narrowed her eyes at him. "Never happening."

"So what, then?"

"Nothing. My dad said he'd bring me dinner tonight. That's all."

Another lie.

Marcos tugged on the strings of his hoodie and looked out toward the street. Her father's car wasn't there. He looked back at the house. Gaby hoped that he didn't notice the ripped window screen. The last thing she needed was him opening his big mouth to everyone about the condition of her home. A month ago, the porch light wasn't working. Marcos told Enrique. The next day, all of Enrique's uncles showed up and turned her house into a day-long project. They fixed the light, unclogged the kitchen sink, chopped the tree branches that hovered dangerously over the porch and power lines, and even took out the trash. She was grateful, but her father came home and acted insulted. He had sulked and muttered, "I was going to get around to it."

Marcos didn't seem to notice her unease. "My mom said I should apologize to you for what I said the other day about that sick cat being kaput. I was just being a jerk. Big surprise."

"You told your mom?" Gaby sat down next to him.

"I tell my mom everything."

Gaby envied him. She used to tell her mom everything, too, but now she could fill a whole notebook with all the things she was keeping from her mom. Like how her father was never home, how she slept on the couch every night, how some girls bullied her after they found out her mom was "illegal" and got deported. Every time her mom called, she wanted to tell her how hard it was, but Gaby didn't want her mom to worry.

"I'm over it." She shrugged.

"Do the owners still want her back?"

"Let's just say the problem has been resolved," Gaby said. "Anyone who leaves their cat at a rest stop shouldn't get it back." Gaby crossed her arms. "That's all."

"Cool." Marcos nodded. "Still feeding the strays, huh?"

"What?" Gaby froze. She looked back at her front door. Did he see Feather? "What are you talking about?"

Marcos shoved the white saucer on the porch with his foot.

"Yeah, that's right," she answered. "They don't come around anymore, though. When my mom is back, I'm sure they'll return."

"Is your mom coming back?"

Gaby's shoulders dropped. "Not you, too." Why was everyone asking her that?

"What do you mean? I'm just sayin'. It's been like forever, you know?"

"*Yes*, I know." She rolled her eyes. Gaby gazed at the big tree in front of her house. Sometimes in the summer, when it was too hot inside the house, Gaby and her mom used to sit on the porch and watch the tree sway in the breeze. Her mom told Gaby about her life in Honduras. How they lived in a house made of cement blocks, plastic bags, and scraps of wood, and how after her mom died, she and her brother struggled to eat. Then her brother got involved with bad people and did bad things for money. She moved in with her aunt, but she felt like a burden. Her aunt was working two jobs and raising three children. Despite her aunt's pleading, Gaby's mom left for the United States, where she hoped she could find work and help her aunt. These memories were like chopping onions. They always made her mom cry.

Now it was Gaby's turn to stare at the tree and cry.

If someone had told Gaby that someday her mom would be taken away from her and she'd have to wait months to see her again, Gaby would never have let her go to work that day. She would have climbed that tree's highest branch and got herself stuck in order to keep her mom home. Marcos watched her like he knew what she was thinking. His hazel eyes usually twinkled between light green and amber, but they were a serious dark green now.

"I dream about her every night. That's how I know she's coming home," Gaby finally said. "It always starts the same. She knocks at the door, but when I open the door she's not there."

"That could mean lots of things. Every detail in a dream

means something. It's like the lines on the palm of your hand. Each tiny line . . . like this, see?" He took her hand and traced a line on her palm. Gaby nodded. "That's like your dream telling you something."

"I think it means my mom will be home soon."

"It means you miss your mom. And if it helps, I miss your mom, too," Marcos said.

Gaby frowned. It was nice to hear, but it didn't help anything.

"Remember how she used to call me Marquito?"

When they were smaller, Gaby's mom watched the four of them after school. That was when her parents were still together. Her mom earned money babysitting and cleaning houses. Gaby had forgotten the affectionate names her mom used for everyone. Alma was "Almita" and Enrique was "Enriquito." It had only been three months since her mom had left. What else had she forgotten about her mom? Gaby bent the edge of her notebook.

"If you read my palm would it tell you when she's coming home?"

"It doesn't work like that," Marcos said.

"What good is it, then?"

"Look, Miss Fussy-Butt, it tells your path, not your mom's path." Marcos rolled his eyes. "You shouldn't worry so much."

Not worry? That was like asking her not to grow fingernails. She worried she'd never see her mom again. She
worried about her dad losing his job. She worried about
bullies like Dolores and Jan. She worried about being a
stray with no mom, no father, no home, no best friend, and
no way to take care of Feather. The only thing that could
make all that go away was her mom coming back once and
for all.

"I'm going to wait here with you until your dad gets
home, okay?"

"You don't have to do that," Gaby said. She wanted to get
back to Feather.

"I have some new card tricks." He smiled and pulled a
pack of cards out of his jacket pocket.

"I have a better idea." Gaby opened her notebook. "No
phony British accent required." Marcos chuckled. She sat up
straight and read Finch's profile.

FINCH

I am a three-year-old male Labrador/shepherd mix. My best buddy Atticus and I were transferred to Furry Friends Animal Shelter from another shelter because we needed more outdoor play space. We are great outdoor explorers! For us, trees are fortresses that must be defended from squirrels. Bones are treasures that must be buried for safety. Rubber balls, Frisbees, and sticks are our rewards. My dream is that Atticus and I can be adopted together so that the adventure will never stop. If you have enough yard space for the both of us, visit Furry Friends Animal Shelter and take us to your castle today!

"That's a good one." Marcos gave her a fist bump. "It's getting late. C'mon, I'll give you a ride to Alma's house."

"My dad will be home any minute."

"You can use my phone and tell him you waited." Marcos extended his cell phone to her.

Gaby didn't like to be home alone, but she wasn't alone anymore. She had Feather now. Plus, she wasn't sure she could face Alma right now. She had said things she didn't mean. "No, it's okay."

"You're stubborn, you know?" Before he got up, he grabbed her hand and squeezed it tight. "Everything is going to be all right, Gaby."

She nodded, but felt like crying again. She'd known Marcos forever. If he said everything was going to be all right, she wanted to believe him, but how could anything be all right?

He got on his bike. "If you change your mind, call me." Marcos jumped off the curb and pedaled away.

Gaby went inside and found Feather curled up into a ball, asleep on her mattress. She spread out her comforter to cover the sleeping cat. The comforter was the last birthday gift from her mom. Gaby had seen the bright purple-and-orange floral comforter at Kmart and loved it. She remembered how her mom inspected the price tag and frowned. The next day, she put it on layaway. Now, the comforter was the only thing that helped Gaby sleep.

While Feather purred, Gaby sat at the dinner table and dug a fork into the enchiladas Marcos had brought. She hadn't eaten since lunch. Even cold, they were the best cheese enchiladas she'd ever tasted. Before she knew it, the plastic container was empty.

Chapter 19

Gaby woke up to banging. Her bedroom door was open, which was strange. She was pretty sure she'd closed it last night. She got up and walked to the doorway of the kitchen. Her dad, dressed in a wrinkled gray T-shirt and jeans, opened and slammed shut the cabinets. He was talking on his cell phone.

"Look, she's fine. I'm taking care of her and she's getting along . . ." He slammed another cabinet. "You need to stop worrying about her —"

"Who are you talking to?" Gaby rubbed her eyes. She looked at the clock on the stove. It was eight thirty.

He turned around and gave her a quick glance. "She's up. You want to talk to her?"

Gaby grabbed for the phone. "Is it Mom? Let me talk to her." He passed her the phone.

"Mom?"

"*Buenos días*, Gaby! How did you sleep?"

"I slept fine. Everyone wants to know when you're coming home."

"I'm sorry, *princesa*. I still don't have enough money —"

"Oh." Gaby's heart sank. "I thought Mr. and Mrs. Gomez sent you money?"

"They did, but I met a coyote and he said I need more for him to get me on a train. I'm working as hard as I can, but jobs don't pay here like they do in the States. You understand that, right?"

Gaby did understand. In the States, her mom made more for a full day of work at the factory than she did during an entire week in Honduras.

Suddenly her father yelled at her from the kitchen. "Where did the last can of tuna go?"

Gaby gasped. Yesterday, she had opened the last can of tuna for Feather. It was still in the basement. *Feather!* Gaby spun around and rushed back to her room with the phone still pressed to her face. Where was she? She scanned her room and looked under her bed. No sign of her.

"Gaby, you understand, right?" her mom asked again.

"Yes, Mom." Gaby walked to the living room, still searching for Feather. "Mom, I got to go."

"Is everything all right? Is your dad taking care of you?"

"Yes. Love you. Miss you."

"I was hoping to hear another one of your animal profiles."

"I'll read you one later. First, I have to do something."

"Okay, *te extraño mucho*, Gaby."

"I miss you more." Gaby hung up the phone. "Did you open my door?" she asked her dad.

"I might have," he grumbled. "Alma's mom called me. She said you didn't stay there last night. I got home late and expected to find you on the couch, but you were in your bed. I don't think I've seen you sleep in your room since I moved in. So, why aren't you at Alma's?"

"I don't . . . uh . . . really know . . ." Gaby answered absently as she searched the dining and living room. There was an odor that reminded her of the shelter. She followed her nose until she saw it. There it was. In the corner of the living room was a puddle. She was close on Feather's trail.

Gaby darted to the bathroom, unfurled half a roll of toilet paper, and came back out. She looked toward the kitchen.

Her father's back was to her and he was pouring a glass of milk. She bent down, wiped up the puddle, and flushed the paper down the toilet. She returned with a can of lemon-scented air freshener and sprayed it around.

"What are you doing that for?"

Gaby sprayed a few more times. "What? This?"

He guzzled milk and then put the glass on the counter with a loud, empty thud. "Yeah, that."

"I can smell your cigarettes."

It was partly true. He didn't smoke inside, but his clothes always carried the smoke smell indoors. She was relieved when he didn't say anything and turned his back to her again. She put the can down on the recliner when she spotted Feather's tail sticking out from under the couch.

"Feather!" Gaby whispered. She got down on her stomach and was about to grab Feather when her father suddenly stood over her.

"What are you doing?"

Gaby popped up from the floor and sat against the couch to cover Feather's tail.

"I . . . I'm looking for tuna. I thought you wanted me to look for tuna." She prayed Feather didn't come out from under the couch just yet.

"Why would it be under the couch?" He frowned a moment, then turned abruptly. "Forget it. I got to get going.

I quit my job last night and I'm meeting a guy about a new one."

"What happened? Why did you quit?"

"Doesn't matter. I'll pick something up to eat on the way. I have to run." He walked to his bedroom.

Gaby mumbled, "I need a snack, too. Is breakfast too much to ask for?" She got down on her stomach again and pulled Feather out from under the couch. Feather meowed. "Shush, sweetie. I got you."

"So why aren't you at Alma's house?" her father yelled from his room. Gaby looked over her shoulder. The coast was clear. She scampered to her room and tossed Feather onto the bed. She closed the door just in time. He came out buttoning a long-sleeve blue shirt. "Did you two get into an argument?"

Gaby shook her head. "No," she mumbled. She and Alma had their disagreements, but they had never argued like they did yesterday. She just wanted to forget the whole thing.

"Did you see the flyers I left for you on the table?"

"Yeah, but I've told you before we're not getting no dogs or cats, Gaby. I can barely feed you and me. Things are tight."

This was his typical rant. Gaby waited for him to take a breath.

"I wrote those for our school's service project. I only wanted you to see them."

"Oh." His voice lightened a little. "I thought you were asking for a pet." He grabbed the keys from the dining room table. "I left five dollars on the kitchen counter for you. Go to Alma's house."

His keys rattled as he locked the front door behind him. The truck coughed a few times, and then roared down the street. She knew he wouldn't be back anytime soon.

CHAPTER 20

Gaby whipped up two scrambled eggs in a skillet. She added the remaining tuna to the eggs to make her specialty, eggs a la tuna. Since she was mostly on her own for breakfast and dinner, she developed a knack for inventing new dishes with food from the City Harvest Center. And even though her own stomach burned from hunger, Gaby put the eggs in a bowl for Feather. The cat sniffed at the eggs and tuna, nudged them with her nose, and then finished them off in a few bites. She meowed for more.

"An eggs a la tuna lover, eh?" Gaby rubbed Feather behind the ears. "We're out of eggs and tuna, I'm sorry. Let's see what else we can find." She searched the cabinets. Feather jumped onto the counter and let her tail thump against it. There were a couple cans of creamed corn, a jar of peanut butter, and a bag of spaghetti. Gaby considered making another specialty of hers, spaghetti a la peanut butter, but decided against it. She was pretty sure she had read somewhere that peanut butter was impossible to get out of whiskers.

"Time to go to the store." She stuffed the five dollars her father left her into her pocket. She took Feather to her bedroom. "Be back soon, Feather." She shut the bedroom door behind her.

On Saturday mornings, Gaby and Alma would usually eat breakfast with Alma's parents, grab their homework, and head to the public library with Alma's mom or jump on bikes and ride around the neighborhood. Today was definitely bike weather. Then it dawned on Gaby that she might bump into Marcos and Enrique riding their bikes. They'd ask her where she was going and what was she doing. She hoped that they were at the Parkway Bridge practicing their wheelies and hops. Underneath the Parkway Bridge was the kids' secret spot to try out tricks on their skateboards or bikes, but it wasn't safe. Cars whizzed by above, and on the other side was a wooded area that Gaby was sure was home to creepy-crawly snakes. It was also where people were known to dump unwanted animals. There was even an official city sign there that said NO DUMPING. It might as well have been written in Latin. It didn't stop anything.

As Gaby walked past several homes, the aroma of eggs, chorizo, and tortillas drifted out and stopped her cold in her tracks. As her stomach let out one loud growl after another, she walked slower to savor the familiar smell that used to pour from her home when her mom was there. She knew that three blocks away, Alma and her family were probably eating the same thing. Gaby lowered her head and picked up her pace. She couldn't think about that right now. Feather depended on her, and she couldn't leave her alone for too long.

When she reached the small neighborhood store, the owner, Mr. Valdivia, was behind the counter reading a magazine.

He looked up. *"Buenos días."*

"Good morning," Gaby answered. The store smelled like Pine-Sol floor cleaner and sold everything from corn tortillas to coconut *paletas*, her favorite fruit ice pop, but it only had two choices for cat litter. Both were more than five dollars. She skimmed over the canned cat food and had just picked up a can of Divine Feline, with a stunning Siamese on the label, when she heard the store's door open and Enrique's voice. She dipped down and peered through the cans of cat food toward the front of the store. Enrique hovered at the front counter and chatted in Spanish with Mr. Valdivia.

That's strange, Gaby thought. On a nice day like today, she was sure Enrique and Marcos would be together. If Marcos wasn't with her and Alma heading to the library, he was always with Enrique. Would Marcos and Alma go to the library together without her? If they did, it would be the first time. She shook her head. It served her right. She should have called and apologized to Alma.

Suddenly, Gaby felt two strong hands on her shoulders. She screamed and dropped the cat food.

"Got you!" Marcos laughed. Gaby's face went red.

Enrique ran over.

"You should have seen her jump." Marcos picked up the can of cat food that rolled toward his feet.

Gaby pointed at him. "You're a jerk, Marcos," she snarled. "Both of you, jerks!"

"Hey, what did I do?" Enrique said.

"Why are you buying cat food?" Marcos waved the can in front of her.

"I'm not." Gaby's voice was defensive.

Marcos squinted. "Then why did you drop this?"

Gaby's mind went blank. Her eyes darted around the

store for some distraction until a lightbulb went on in her head. "That's it!" she said out loud.

Both boys exchanged confused glances. Enrique scratched his head. "What's going on?"

The cat on the can looked exactly like the chubby Siamese she'd rescued. Mrs. Sepulveda would have cat litter to loan her. "It's not for me," Gaby said. "Mrs. Sepulveda asked me to pick up cat food for her. She's not feeling well." She snatched the can out of his hands and then took two more from the shelf. She scurried up to the counter.

"You sure those aren't for you?" Marcos asked. She ignored him and managed a sweet smile for Mr. Valdivia as he rang up the cat food. "Maybe all your work at the shelter has turned you into a cat?" he said. "And now you crave cat food."

Enrique meowed. She tossed them both a vicious glare over her shoulder. She took her change from Mr. Valdivia and stomped out of the store while both boys continued to meow.

Turning into a cat! Gaby fumed. All of that hand-squeezing-everything-is-going-to-be-all-right talk meant nothing to him. Once Marcos is with Enrique or any other boy he becomes a dog. No, not a dog! Dogs are sweet. Sweet like Cinder, Puck, Bonita, Atticus, and Finch. Marcos is a jerk.

It wasn't until she got to Mrs. Sepulveda's light blue house that she calmed down. In the yard, there was a small statue of St. Francis of Assisi, the patron saint of animals, surrounded by pink rosebushes. Gaby prayed under her breath. "Please, St. Francis, let her be home. Feather is in serious need of cat litter." She rang the doorbell. A cat yowled from inside and steps approached.

"Good morning, Gaby," Mrs. Sepulveda said through the screen door.

It had been a while since Gaby saw Mrs. Sepulveda, and she had more gray hair than she remembered. Ever since Mrs. Sepulveda retired from her work as a university professor, she traveled all the time. "I hope I'm not bothering you." Gaby smiled.

"Of course not — wait a minute, my cat is —" The cat moaned and scratched at the screen door. "Shush, Queen!"

"Is she okay?" Gaby asked.

"Yes, she's fine. It's just whenever I open the door she wants out." She bent down and picked the cat up. "Have you met Queen?"

Gaby nodded and half smiled at the cat that had led her up a tree and left her with welts all over her arm and shoulder. She decided she wouldn't tell Mrs. Sepulveda about how Queen got stuck in the tree in front of her house or the stinging red welts she'd given her.

"Anyway, where are my manners?" she said. "Please come in."

Inside the house, large framed pictures of Mrs. Sepulveda and Queen posed in front of the Statue of Liberty, the Liberty Bell, and the Grand Canyon hung on the walls.

She put Queen down. "How are things, Gaby?" The cat brushed up against Gaby's legs and sniffed.

"Last night a stray cat came to my house, and —"

"Ugh! It's that highway, I tell you. People think they can dump their pets under the bridge. Instead they should get them spayed and neutered. Makes me so angry!" Mrs. Sepulveda raged. Queen and Gaby stared at her. "I'm sorry." Mrs. Sepulveda fanned herself with her hand. "You were saying that you needed some food for your stray?"

"Actually, I bought some food." Gaby pulled a can out from the grocery bag and handed it to Mrs. Sepulveda.

"That's some expensive food, Gaby." She gave the can back.

Gaby nodded. "She needs premium nutrition."

"Of course." Mrs. Sepulveda smiled.

"What I really need is cat litter."

"I have tons of it." She got up and led Gaby to the kitchen. Queen jumped from the floor to the kitchen counter. She strutted with her tail in the air. Every few steps, she'd stop and throw a sparkling, blue-eyed glance at Gaby. When she got to the sink, the Siamese stopped for a drink straight from the faucet. Gaby giggled. Queen was quite the troublemaker. "Get!" Mrs. Sepulveda raised a threatening finger. Queen leaped from the sink to a small breakfast table. She sat next to a large bowl of bananas, apples, and oranges and wrapped her chocolate-dipped tail around it. Gaby had never seen bananas so yellow or apples so bright red. Her stomach growled.

Mrs. Sepulveda pulled out a bag of cat litter from a wicker hamper. "Take this. Queen didn't like it." Queen thumped her tail against the table and mewed. "You're so spoiled." She closed the hamper. "You're actually doing me a favor by getting it off my hands. Do you have a box for the cat litter, dear?"

"I have an old storage container at home."

"That should work." Mrs. Sepulveda nodded. "Now tell me, will you take the cat to a shelter or keep it?"

"Well, I'm not sure. My dad doesn't like cats, but I can't let her starve."

Mrs. Sepulveda stepped closer to Gaby. "You know who you remind me of, don't you?" Gaby shook her head. "Your mom!" She clasped her hands together and smiled. "Your mom was very special and so are you."

Gaby bit down on her bottom lip. She didn't feel special. She had rushed off the phone with her mom this morning. Plus, in the span of a few hours, she had lied to her classmates, Alma, Alma's mother, her father, Marcos, Enrique, and now Mrs. Sepulveda. She knew her mom would not approve.

"Tell me," Mrs. Sepulveda said, "have you talked to your mom lately?"

"Just this morning."

That was the truth, at least.

"Oh, Gaby. I'm still so shocked about that whole ordeal." Mrs. Sepulveda leaned back against the breakfast table. Queen positioned herself under Mrs. Sepulveda's arm. "Queen and I were in New York. I didn't even get to say good-bye to her."

"Mr. Gomez hired a lawyer so that I could spend a little time with her before she left."

"That's what I heard. They are good people." She nodded. "Your mom is a strong woman. I'm willing to bet she is working harder than ever and saving every Honduran *lempira* she can to prepare a good home for you to visit in Honduras. You'd like to visit Honduras, wouldn't you?"

Gaby's eyes watered. Visit? Mrs. Sepulveda's question echoed in Gaby's head like she was the one at the Grand Canyon. No, she didn't want her mom to prepare a home in Honduras. No, she didn't want to visit her mom in Honduras. She wanted her mom to come home.

"I'm sorry, did I say something wrong?" Mrs. Sepulveda grabbed a napkin from the table and handed it to Gaby.

"It's okay . . . it's just . . ." Gaby dabbed her eyes. "I thought my mom would be back by now. She promised, but she's still in Honduras."

"Hmmm." Mrs. Sepulveda's eyebrows rose. "Gaby, it's incredibly tough to cross the border right now. I'm sure you've seen the news about how bad it is, right?"

Gaby nodded. She had seen the news, but it would be different for her mom. It just had to be different. She needed her mom at home with her.

"Well, next time you talk to your mom please let her know that I'm thinking of her and if she needs anything, to not hesitate to ask, all right?"

Mrs. Sepulveda gathered Queen in her arms and walked Gaby out.

"Make sure your stray gets plenty of water. If it's been out in the streets, it's probably dehydrated," Mrs. Sepulveda said.

"Thank you." Gaby waved.

"Wait!" Mrs. Sepulveda called out. Gaby stopped outside the fence. Mrs. Sepulveda disappeared into the house and then returned with an apple and banana. "You're too skinny. Eat these. And good luck with that stray."

CHAPTER 21

As soon as Gaby got home, she opened a can of food for Feather. While Feather ate, Gaby devoured the banana and went to the basement to find a box for the cat litter. She found a transparent plastic container that belonged to her mom. Against Gaby's protests, her father had packed up all of her mother's things when he moved in. It was a big fight. Gaby screamed that her mom would be back, so there was no need to move her stuff to the basement. He had just waited until she was at school and then moved everything downstairs. Gaby didn't speak to him for days.

She opened the plastic container. It was full of notebooks and a few sheets of Spanish songs. Gaby recognized them all. Her favorite song, "*De Colores*," was one that her mom had taught all the kids she babysat. There were also a couple of white doilies with pink and red flowers that her mom made as gifts. Every Christmas, the students brought gifts to their teachers at St. Ann's. Most of the girls gave perfume or scarves, but Gaby couldn't afford to buy gifts. Her mom made homemade presents instead. Last Christmas, Gaby gave her fifth-grade teacher a dozen pork tamales made with plantain leaves. Her teacher liked them so much, she ended up ordering five dozen more for a holiday party. With the extra money, her mom bought Gaby new shoes and a pair of jeans at JCPenney.

Gaby opened an English workbook filled with her mom's writing. Her mom had doodled pretty flowers and birds at the edges of each page. Doodling was something Gaby liked to do, too. She chuckled when she saw a sentence her mom had written: "The house mine is in the hill." Her mom worked on her English every day. By the time she was deported, she could sing along to country music on the radio, read the newspaper, and talk back to the evening news.

Gaby gathered all the doilies, sheet music, and workbooks into a neat pile. She took the empty box. She knew her mom wouldn't mind if she used the container for Feather. At the bottom of the stairs, Gaby heard her father's truck. It coughed and sputtered. Gaby dropped the box and raced up the stairs. She had to hide Feather!

At the top of the stairs, she heard the front door open. It was too late.

"Gaby!" he yelled. "Gaby!" His tone was harsh, and she knew what that meant. She walked into the dining room. Across the room from her, her father's blue eyes were narrowed in on Feather cleaning herself on the dining room table. It would have been cute if she wasn't in so much trouble.

"Why is there a cat on the table?" he growled.

"I . . . uh . . . found her." Gaby leaned forward to reach for Feather, but the cat jumped off and brushed up against her father's legs, meowing. He glowered at the cat. Feather mewed and rubbed her head against his right shoe. He pulled his foot away. Suddenly, Feather lurched forward and spewed a massive gooey glob of chewed-up eggs, dried cat food, and tuna onto her father's shoe.

"Oh, Feather!" Gaby cried. She grabbed a paper towel from the kitchen and rushed to Feather.

"That's disgusting!" her father yelled. He stomped to the bathroom. "Get that cat out of my sight, right now!"

"I'm sorry! She's been sick! It's not her fault! I'll clean your shoe, I promise."

Her father walked out of the bathroom and into his bedroom. "I'm not playing, Gaby. If you don't throw that cat out, I will." From the bedroom, he mumbled and cursed. Gaby was still cleaning Feather's whiskers when he reappeared from his bedroom with a change of shoes.

"But . . . we can't throw her out . . ."

"Oh yes we can, and I will." He plucked Feather up by back of the neck. Feather cried as he headed toward the front door.

Gaby went running after him. "Please no, no!"

He swung the door open and was about to fling Feather outside when Gaby grabbed his arm. "She's not a stray, Dad. She's from the shelter."

He hesitated, then stepped back to glare at Gaby.

"Shelter? What shelter?" Feather still hung from his hand like a bag of trash you take to the alley. "You adopted a cat from a shelter without my permission?"

Gaby's face was hot. Tears streamed down each cheek. "No, she's from the shelter where we volunteer." Gaby wiped tears from her eyes. "My school service project." She sobbed. "I want to keep her."

He screwed up his face then, real tight, like he didn't know whether to explode or walk away. Gaby wiped her nose with her sleeve. Finally her dad shook his head. "You're not keeping a cat while I'm here in this house! It's going back right now. Take it and let's go." He shoved Feather into Gaby's arms, pulled the front door open, and stomped down the porch steps.

Gaby held Feather close. "What are we going to do now?" she said weakly. Feather mewed softly. Gaby looked through the screen door at the truck. Her dad sat behind the wheel smoking a cigarette. He honked the horn.

Gaby wiped her nose on her sleeve once more, and then went out to the truck. She had barely sat down in the front seat with Feather and shut the door when her dad sped off.

Chapter 22

Gaby's father's eyes narrowed and his knuckles tightened around the steering wheel. She was certain that this wasn't the same father that had held her hand so many years ago when she was frightened by cockroaches. This father smelled like cigarettes and scowled at the road. Feather lay limp on Gaby's lap.

While petting her, Gaby sang soft and slow, *"De colores, de colores, se visten los campos en la primavera . . ."* Feather lifted her head and gazed up at Gaby, and she sang, *"De colores, de colores, son los pajaritos que vienen de afuera —"*

"You guys go all this way for a volunteer project?"

"It's only fifteen minutes from our school. Take the next right, at the light," Gaby instructed.

He was quiet for a minute, and then looked over at the cat with disgust.

"Please, Dad, we can't take her back."

"Give me one good reason why not."

"I love her and I want to take care of her."

"You can't *love* a cat," he scoffed.

"I do." She kissed Feather's head. In return, Feather sat up and rubbed her face against Gaby's cheek. "Please."

He rolled his eyes. "She'll be better off at the shelter. We can't take care of her."

"Well, then, you should leave me at the shelter, too, because you don't take care of *me*."

"What are you talking about?" He stomped on the brakes at a red light, and they lurched forward. "We're talking about a cat."

"What about you?" Gaby blurted. "You don't even come home, or pay the bills. If it wasn't for Alma's family, I'd probably starve."

"Don't exaggerate."

"You don't ask how I'm doing. You don't ask about school or how I feel about Mom or if I need anything. You don't care!"

"That's enough!"

It was quiet. He rubbed his forehead and mumbled to himself. The light turned green. The shelter loomed ahead.

"Dad," she tried again, "if you're mad at me then be mad at me, but, please, I have to save her."

He turned into the lot and parked. "There's nothing I can do about it."

"That's the same thing you say about Mom." She got out of the truck with Feather, slammed the door, and marched up to the shelter.

She didn't recognize the woman behind the reception desk. Where was Daisy? She looked up at the clock on the wall. It was past one o'clock. Maybe Daisy was out for lunch?

She stepped up to the desk, but before she could speak the woman smiled wide. "Feather! Dr. Villalobos is going to be so happy!" She got on the phone. "Dr. V., Feather is back."

Gaby wiped her eyes some more. She had no idea what she would say to Dr. V. Feather meowed. "Don't worry. Everything's going to be okay." Through the front window, she saw her dad finish a cigarette and head toward the shelter.

"Gaby?" Dr. Villalobos said. "Wow, I didn't expect to see you." He squatted down in front of her and petted Feather. He shook his head. "I don't understand. How did you find her?"

"I didn't." Gaby took a deep breath. "I took her from the shelter when no one was looking."

Her father walked in. Dr. Villalobos stood and put out his hand.

"Hi, can I help you?"

"I'm Gaby's dad." The men shook hands. Gaby's dad was tall, but Dr. Villalobos still towered above him. "She brought this cat home and we're bringing it back."

Gaby buried her face in Feather's fur.

"Don't know how she got this cat," her dad continued. "But I can't afford it. Don't care for cats, really."

Gaby glared at her father.

"That's my fault," Dr. Villalobos said. "I asked her to take the cat home."

Gaby almost gasped in surprise. She'd kidnapped his cat and now he was coming to her rescue? It didn't make sense. He pulled her to his side and gave her shoulder a reassuring squeeze. "I wanted to see if the cat could handle being in a house with a family."

Her father rolled his eyes. "She said she had to save it."

Gaby's heart stopped.

Dr. Villalobos looked pained for a minute. "Well, yes, we send cats home so they can be saved. I'm sure that's what she meant."

"Well, whatever. You should check with the parents

before you send kids home with cats." Gaby's father turned and walked toward the door. "If you'll take the cat back, I got to get going." He pulled the car keys out of his front pocket.

"But Dad —" Gaby whimpered.

"If you'll give us a few minutes," Dr. Villalobos interrupted, "Gaby can help me get the cat settled." He took Feather from Gaby. As they walked to the clinic, Dr. V. was quiet.

Gaby took a good look around. She was certain that this would be the last time she'd be allowed into the shelter. Her days at Furry Friends Animal Shelter were over.

Chapter 23

Dr. Villalobos opened the clinic door. "Daisy thought she'd left a door open and that Feather had escaped. She went home in tears last night." He put Feather on the examination table. "Why did you take her, Gaby?"

"I'm sorry." She hung her head. "You told me that Feather's owners threatened to sue you. Feather deserves a better family."

"I see." He pressed his hands along Feather's ribs.

"What happens now? Are you going to tell Mrs. Kohler?"

He checked Feather's ears. "I wish I didn't have to, but I do." Gaby met his eyes and then burst into fresh tears. Feather meowed.

"If you tell Mrs. Kohler, I won't be allowed back to the shelter." Dr. V. handed her a tissue. "I'm really sorry. I couldn't let Feather be with those people. They don't care about her." She blew her nose.

"I know." Dr. V. nodded. "But Mrs. Kohler trusts me and I have to tell her the truth." He examined Feather's eyes and mouth. "Look, I'm not happy about it either. I might lose my shelter scribe," he said. "I'll talk to her. Maybe she'll still let you volunteer."

Gaby wiped her nose. "I'd do anything."

"The way I see it," Dr. Villalobos said, "you thought you were saving Feather. If I thought a dog or cat was in danger, I'd do the same thing."

"Even lie?"

"Well, it's never right to lie," he said. "One lie traps you into more lies."

"You lied. You covered for me with my dad."

"You got me there, kiddo. Your dad looked upset. I didn't think the truth under those circumstances was worth it. Your eyes were all puffy and red."

Gaby nodded. "He would have flipped out even more if he knew I took Feather."

"When I was about your age, my brothers and I hid a dog and her entire litter of pups in the garage. My dad was a real tough guy. Worked long hours at construction and always came home exhausted and sore. We thought that if he found out, he'd dump them for sure. It turned out he was a bigger dog lover than me. He played fetch with them every free moment he had." Dr. Villalobos pointed to a tattoo on his arm. "My first tattoo, see?"

On his forearm was a tattoo of a large dog surrounded by six small pups and the name "Princess Leia."

Gaby shook her head and smiled.

"Well, what do you expect from three boys? We named them after *Star Wars* characters." He shrugged. "Lucky for all of us, Feather looks good. Did she eat anything? Did you give her water?"

"Yes, I fed her Divine Feline, eggs a la tuna, and I gave her lots of water, but she vomited on my dad's shoe."

"Yikes! Not a good first impression." Dr. Villalobos smiled.

"Will she be okay?"

"Most likely she got sick from the change in diet. She's not used to that sort of rich food. Also, the stress of being in a new place could cause her to regurgitate. Feather is a strong cat to have survived on her own for as long as she did, but she's still fragile."

Gaby bit down on her lip. All this time, she thought she was saving Feather, but in reality she was no different than Feather's former owners. She'd stressed Feather out and made her sick by feeding her eggs a la tuna and Divine Feline. Dr. V. picked Feather up and stroked her back.

"Don't worry, she'll be fine. And I'll make sure Mrs. Kohler knows what good care you gave her." Still holding Feather, Dr. V. pulled a chair out for Gaby. "Come sit for a minute. I need to tell you something." He sat across from her.

Gaby knew enough about adults to know that when they wanted to be at eye level and started talking softly, it meant they wanted to be serious. She had heard that tone of voice before. Softness hiding something hard. Mrs. Kohler used that voice when she announced exams. Three months ago, the lawyer used it when he told Gaby and Alma's family that there was nothing else that could be done to keep her mom in the country.

"Feather's owners didn't come to pick her up, but they called and said they'd come tomorrow. If they really want Feather back, there's nothing I can do." If Gaby had any tears left in her body they would have poured out, but she could only muster a gasp.

"I'd hoped they'd lose interest, but they haven't."

"Furry Friends has a waiting list policy, Dr. V. If there is another family on the list first, they'd have to wait, right?"

"That's right. The only thing is . . . Feather's been in the clinic, so I don't have anybody on her waiting list. I won't be able to justify keeping her."

"Put my name on the waiting list! When my mom is back, we'll adopt her," Gaby said.

"When will your mom be back?"

"She promised she'd be home soon," Gaby said.

"Unless your mom can be back by tomorrow, I'm afraid I have no choice."

"But they can't be trusted," Gaby cried. "They left her at a rest stop."

"I will have a long talk with them."

Gaby felt a lump rise in her throat.

Dr. V. stood up. "You should get back to your dad. I've kept you too long, and he seemed anxious to leave."

"Can I hold Feather one more time, just in case I don't get to see her again?"

Gaby took Feather and embraced her. It reminded her of that last day she saw her mom. In the airport, her mom kissed Gaby's forehead and told her, "We'll be together again." Even though every bone in Gaby's body ached and her heart crumbled like the Mexican cookies Alma's mother made for Cinco de Mayo, her mom's kiss and her words calmed her. She just had to be patient.

Back in the reception area, Gaby's father sat on a chair with his eyes closed. She tapped his shoulder. "Ready?"

Once in the truck, her father started the engine and then stopped. "We need to talk, Gaby. There's going to be some changes."

Gaby's heart raced. All this catnapping hadn't solved anything. It had only made things worse. She and Alma had gotten into a big fight, Feather's owners were coming tomorrow, her volunteering days were over, and now her father wanted to talk to her about changes. What changes? He pulled the keys out of the ignition and twisted around to face her. "I got a new job today. It's in Dodge City." He exhaled. "This means we're moving."

"What? Dodge City? That's really far away . . . What about Mom?" Gaby clutched the door handle.

"First of all, do you realize how impossible it is for your mom to come back home? It's not going to happen. The faster you get that through your head, the better."

"What do you mean? She told me —"

"Do you remember a few weeks ago, when you woke up and heard me on the phone?"

Gaby remembered that night perfectly. He had been hunched over the table, whispering into the phone. Then, when she woke up, he'd hung up really fast.

"I was talking to your mom. She was calling to ask me for money to pay a coyote. I told her I wouldn't send her any because it wasn't worth the risk."

Her father's words stung. Why wouldn't he help her mom? Was he saying she wasn't worth it?

"No matter how good of a coyote they may have, people don't just waltz over the border. Do you understand that? It's dangerous. You need to stop pleading with her to come home. It's not safe."

She couldn't believe it. Why was he saying this? There was no way she was moving anywhere with him. She gazed back at the shelter, wishing her father would just plop her in a box and leave her at the door.

CHAPTER 24

Gaby stomped straight to her room.

"I'm not going anywhere without my mom!" She slammed the door behind her, snatched her mom's photo off the dresser, and collapsed on her bed. "Especially not to Dodge-whatever with *you*!"

Her father paced outside her door before he finally knocked. "Gaby, come out so we can talk."

"If you want to leave, leave already! It's never stopped you before!" she cried.

"Okay, this has gone on too long. Let's call your mom."

Gaby sat up and rushed out of her bedroom to find him already dialing.

"It's ringing. Do you want to talk to her?"

Gaby crossed her arms and glared so hard her face hurt. "Of course I want to talk to her."

"Paloma, it's me. I have Gaby here and — you need to talk to her —"

"Mom?" Gaby grabbed for the phone, but her father stepped away. She couldn't wait to tell her mom about her dad's plan to take her to Dodge City. There's no way her mom would go for that. No way.

"Paloma, she thinks you can just stroll across the border." Gaby could barely make out her mother's voice. She sounded upset. Her father held the phone out to her. "Talk to her."

Gaby grabbed the phone. Her entire body shook. "Mom?" Gaby said. "Dad said you're not coming back and he wants me to move to Dodge City with him."

"I'm sorry, *princesa*."

Gaby's legs wobbled and her chest tightened. Somehow, she found a chair and sat down. "What?" She shook her head. This was not the reaction she was expecting from her mom. "No, you have to tell him he's wrong. You're coming back." Gaby heard deep breathy sobs on the other end of the line. "Mom?"

"*Princesa*, I want to return, but . . ." Her mom stopped, blew her nose. Gaby felt tears slip from her eyes. "Listen to

155

me, Gaby. I've been working and saving as much as I can, but I just can't make enough to come home right now. I've been working so hard, and I've had to use most of what I earn for my aunt's medical treatments. She's very sick."

"What?" Gaby cried. "What about me?"

"I'm so sorry." Her mom's voice trembled. Gaby covered her face with her hands. Was this it? Was she never going to see her mom again? How could this happen? Her heart felt like it would burst into a million pieces.

"Are you saying you're not even going to try?" Gaby pressed.

"Gaby, *mi princesa*, you have to be patient —"

"No, Mom! I've been patient. I've been patient for three months! And stop calling me your *princesa*. If I were your *princesa*, you'd be here. You said before that I was worth the journey. I'm your daughter and I want you to come back! You promised!"

"Gaby!" Her father pounded the table with his fist, but she ignored him.

She slammed the phone down.

The silence that followed sent a sharp pain through Gaby's whole body. How could she hang up on her mom? She ran out the front door. Her father yelled after her, but she wasn't stopping.

Chapter 25

Gaby ran until she got to Marcos's house. His bike leaned against the front porch. She went around back and threw pebbles at his window until he finally looked out. She gestured for him to meet her in the garage.

His mother's red Charger was parked inside the garage. Even though cars didn't interest Gaby, she knew that this was a classic old car. So when she entered the car on the driver's side she tried not to touch anything. She stared at the rosary that dangled from the rearview mirror. Gaby had prayed the rosary a hundred times when her mom was detained. She had prayed for a miracle. She'd showed up every day during visiting hours, clutching a rosary so that the officers would see that her mom had a daughter who wanted her home.

Marcos jumped in on the passenger side.

"Are we going for a ride?" he quipped. Gaby wiped her eyes with the back of her hand. "Hey, what's wrong?"

"I need you to read my palm." She shoved her right hand at him. He had predicted that the girls would volunteer at Furry Friends Animal Shelter. He had told her he could see a person's path in life through the lines of the palm. Where did her path lead? And was her mom with her on that same path?

He backed up. "What's going on?"

"Please, just read my palm."

Marcos took her hand and peered closer. "Let me see . . . You have a strong life and head line on your right palm. Let me see your left." He took her left hand in his. "You have deep lines on both hands."

"What does that mean?"

"Deep lines mean a strong soul."

"I don't care about that. I need to know if I'm moving or not."

"I'm sorry. I don't see travel — what's going on, Gaby?"

"Thanks for nothing!" She got out of the car, slammed the door, and ran through the alley. She headed straight to the Parkway Bridge. She wished she could run to Alma, but she knew that was out of the question. Her father was probably already at Alma's house, calling her an ungrateful brat.

Gaby ran until she fell on a soft spot of grass under a tree. She sat down, leaned back against the tree, and listened to the cars zoom over the bridge. If there were creepy-crawly snakes or mice in the high grass, she didn't care anymore. Nothing could hurt worse than knowing her mom wasn't coming back.

It was so unfair. Other people had their moms and dads. Why did it have to be so hard for her? She wished her mom had never left and that everything could be the same as it used to be.

An engine roared from behind her. She turned to face the noise. A pickup truck pulled over along the curb and parked. She slinked down. If it was her father, then that meant someone — Alma or Marcos — had told him about the Parkway Bridge.

Gaby hoped it wasn't her father. She knew she couldn't stay out all night, but she didn't want to face her dad just yet either.

A short, stocky man got out of the truck. It was definitely not her father. Suddenly, Gaby felt scared. She was all by herself, and no one knew where she was. Gaby thought of her mom. Was this what it was like when she had traveled to the United States? Her mom had been so alone and scared. Now, Gaby was scared, too.

The man lifted a duffle bag out of the back of the truck and began shaking it out. What was he doing? That's when Gaby heard high-pitched yelps. For the hundredth time that day, Gaby's heart pounded. Once the man was done, he threw the bag into the back of the truck, got behind the wheel, and drove off.

She crept toward the cries. She was about to take one more step when she saw a tiny black kitten at her feet. Gaby picked it up. It was as small as the palm of her hand. She counted five more squirming and mewing on the ground. "It's okay, kitties." It was unbelievable that someone would just abandon kittens as young as these. The next thing Gaby knew, she was trading the kitten for a rock and running after the truck.

"What kind of monster are you?" She threw the rock. The truck was still in sight, but too far away for her rock to get anywhere near it. She picked up another one. "You can't just dump animals" — she threw the rock — "and leave them alone out here!" She launched another. Gaby kicked dirt and gravel up until she lost her footing and fell hard on the ground. She would have stayed there, if it wasn't for the sound of the tiny kittens mewing.

They sounded more like small birds than cats. Gaby got up and dusted herself off. Carefully, she scanned the ground and gathered the kittens one by one into a nearby cardboard box. "It's okay, *gatitos*." She sat down on the grass. Her head hurt. "You're with me now."

A sound of metal screeched. "Gaby!" Alma yelled.

Gaby raised a free hand and shouted back, "Over here!"

Alma and Marcos jumped off their bikes and raced to Gaby's side. Alma shook her head and grabbed a kitten. "Why is it that every time I find you in trouble, there's a cat involved?" She stroked the kitten with her fingertips.

"I know. It's crazy," Gaby managed to say. "Some man dumped them . . . like they were nothing."

Marcos took a couple of kittens and kissed their heads. "We heard about everything, Gaby," he said.

"No one blames you," Alma added. "Your dad came over to our house. He was really upset. Then my parents got upset at him. Then my parents called your mom and she was upset that you ran off and —"

"Basically, every adult we know is freaking out. She gets it, Alma," Marcos interrupted. Gaby gave a weak smile. Marcos and Alma. Her heart felt sore. She didn't want to move to Dodge City with her father. It was bad enough her mom was never coming home; she didn't want to lose her best friends, too.

"Alma, I'm so sorry about what I said. I didn't mean it. I love your family."

"Aha! I knew you guys were fighting," Marcos said.

"Really?" Alma snapped at him.

"Do you forgive me, Alma?" Gaby asked.

"Only if you forgive me, too."

"Hug it out! Hug it out!" Marcos directed. The girls hugged.

"We've got to get you and these precious kittens home," Alma said. "Are you ready to come home?"

"Home? Where is that?" Gaby choked up. "My dad is moving us to Dodge City."

Alma helped Gaby up on her feet. "I have a better idea. You have to tell your dad that you want to move in with my family. It's what you want, right?"

"You two in the same *casa*?" Marcos shook his head and whistled. "There goes the neighborhood."

"It's what I want, but my dad will never go for it."

"You have to try to convince him, Gaby."

Gaby looked down at the small kittens in the flimsy cardboard box. She had thrown rocks at a stranger for them. She had smuggled Feather out of the shelter to save her. If she could do all that, maybe she did have the strength to tell her dad that she didn't want to go to Dodge City, and maybe this time he'd listen.

Chapter 26

When they reached Alma's house, pizza covered one end of the dining room table. The aroma of pepperoni made Gaby's mouth water. Except for the fruit Mrs. Sepulveda gave her earlier, she hadn't eaten anything all day.

Alma ran to the basement to find a sturdier box and old towels for the kittens' bed, almost crashing into her mom as she came out of the kitchen.

"Sweet Gaby, we were so worried." She kissed Gaby's forehead. "But I see you found some friends."

"Actually, they found me." Gaby handed her a kitten.

"Newborns!" Mrs. Gomez exclaimed. "So precious!"

"Some dude dumped them at the Parkway Bridge," Marcos said.

"What a creep!" Mrs. Gomez exclaimed. She kissed the kitten and took it to the couch. "I'd like to dump him. Give him some of his own medicine. What do you say about that, *gatita*?" Mrs. Gomez held the kitten close to her chest. "Cats this young shouldn't be separated from their mom." She looked up suddenly at Gaby. "How are you holding up?"

"I'll survive." Gaby shrugged. "Can we take them to the shelter tomorrow? Dr. Villalobos will know what to do."

"That's a good idea." She tucked a loose strand of Gaby's hair behind her ear. "Your dad was here earlier, but he left to go look for you. I want to call him to let him know you're safe, okay?"

Gaby nodded. "Did Mr. Gomez go with him?"

"No, Mr. Gomez went on his bike to ride around and talk to neighbors in case someone saw you." She picked up her cell phone and walked to the dining room table. Gaby dreaded seeing her dad. He had already freaked out about one cat. What was he going to say about a whole litter?

Alma returned with towels and a box. They set up a bed for the kittens. Gaby wished she could go to bed and then wake up to find that the entire day had just been a bad dream and her mom was on her way home.

Mrs. Gomez got off the phone and yelled for them to start eating. Alma grabbed glasses filled with ice cubes and her mom put a pitcher of lemonade on the table. All of them took a seat and divvied up slices of pizza. Mr. Gomez came home just as Gaby was taking her first cheesy bite. He went around the table and kissed each of them on the top of their heads before sitting down.

"Your dad said he was glad you're safe," Mrs. Gomez said.

"Is he coming over?"

Mrs. Gomez exchanged a worried look with Mr. Gomez. "I talked to him. He said he had some things to do tonight."

Gaby's head dropped. Was her father even worried about her? She took a deep breath. Mr. Gomez reached out and patted Gaby's hand.

Between bites of pizza, Gaby apologized for lying, and told them what happened with Feather at home, about her visits with Mrs. Sepulveda and Dr. V., and her talk with her mom.

"All this time, I've been waiting for my mom to come home and then she tells me I have to be more patient. And meanwhile, my dad wants to drag me to Dodge City." Even though her stomach growled, Gaby ignored the second slice of pizza on her plate.

"No one cares about what I want." She scooted back from the table. "I'm sorry, I can't eat anymore." She got up from the table and walked outside to the playground set that she'd played on since she and Alma were children. She climbed the ladder to the slide and sat at the top.

Alma's family had bought the swing set on Alma's fifth birthday. The day it arrived, all the parents, including Gaby's mom and dad, gathered to put it together. Once it was done, the children played for hours while the adults grilled hamburgers, talked, and listened to music that made everyone's hips move. For years, Alma's backyard was the hit of the neighborhood. Gaby and every kid on the block had gone down the slide, and Alma and Marcos had banged up their knees hundreds of times jumping off the swings in midair.

A few minutes later, Alma and Marcos came outside and sat down on the swings. Gaby was grateful that they didn't speak to her or try to make her explain how she felt. They swung in silence. Then, from inside the house, the phone rang. A lump as big as a mango formed in Gaby's throat. It rang twice before Mrs. Gomez came to the back door and called for Gaby. "Your mom is on the phone. She wants to talk to you."

Gaby sat frozen. Alma and Marcos stopped swinging. She could feel their eyes.

For months, she had raced to the phone to talk to her mom. Now, she didn't want to hear what her mom had to say. She didn't want to hear she wasn't coming home.

"Gaby?" Alma said.

"Tell her I don't want to talk," she said.

Mrs. Gomez hesitated as if she wanted to say something, but she didn't. She went inside.

"Why did you do that?" Marcos asked.

She took a deep breath. "From now on I'm going to decide," Gaby said softly, "what's best for me." Gaby closed her eyes and slid down.

chapter 27

On the way to the shelter, Gaby dozed in and out of sleep. She had spent most of the night tossing and turning. Ever since her mother had been deported, it was usually question after question that kept her awake. Now, Gaby had answers, and she could respond to those questions like she was taking a true-and-false exam at school.

I. **Gaby's mom will be home soon.**
   False! In fact, her mom is never coming back. Ever.

2. **Gaby's father will find a good job.**

   True! Her father found a new job in a new city and is moving three hundred miles away.

She moved closer to Alma to look at the box of kittens on her lap. The kittens were snuggled tight against one another. *They* had no problem sleeping.

"Your mom called again before we left the house," Alma's mother said from the driver's seat. "She really wants to talk to you. When do you think you'll be ready to talk to her?"

Gaby petted the kittens. "I don't know."

They turned into the Furry Friends Animal Shelter parking lot. Dr. V. greeted them wearing a bright Japanese anime T-shirt. "You're here!" he sang. Gaby suddenly felt happier.

Dr. V. introduced himself to Alma's parents and gave Alma and Gaby a hug.

"Is Feather still here, Dr. V.?" Gaby asked.

"Yep, her former owners haven't shown up yet and I close early on Sundays." He took the box of kittens from Alma. "So if they're not here by four o'clock, they're out of luck, which will be the third time they've failed to pick her up."

Gaby shot Alma a hopeful look. "Maybe they've forgotten about her."

"They've done it before," Alma said.

Alma took her parents to Spike's cage outside. When Dr. V. and Gaby entered the clinic, Gaby rushed to Feather's cage, but Feather wasn't there.

She gasped. "Where is Feather?"

"She's in the cat room."

"But that . . . that would mean . . . Feather could be adopted by anyone."

He gently placed the newborns into a crate lined with a soft blanket. "These kitties are lucky you found them."

Gaby went to help him. "Dr. V., what's going on? Why is Feather in the cat room?"

"I was thinking about what you said. You know, about you and your mom adopting Feather . . ."

Gaby's stomach churned.

"I put Feather in the cat room so that she could be adopted, and guess whose name is at the top of the waiting list?"

"Mine?"

"Yep!"

Gaby gazed at the newborns and frowned.

Dr. V. watched her. "What's wrong? I expected at least a high five."

Gaby sat down on the office chair. "My mom isn't coming home."

"Why? What's going on?"

She wasn't sure if she should tell him. There were some people, like Dolores and Jan, who disliked people like her mom. Still, she knew Dr. V. was nothing like Dolores and Jan.

"I don't want you to think bad about my mom, but before I was born my mom snuck into the country. You know, without legal papers?" Gaby glanced up to see Dr. Villalobos's reaction.

"Go on. What happened?" he asked.

"Three months ago, immigration raided her work. She wasn't even supposed to be there that day. It was her day off, but she was covering for a woman who had a sick baby at home. They deported her and now she says it's too dangerous to make the trip back." Gaby looked down at her hands. "So we won't be able to save Feather, Dr. V. You'll have to find someone else to adopt her. Someone who will love her the way I do."

Dr. Villalobos crossed his arms. "Feather will be fine. Cats always land on their feet. I'm worried about you" — he pulled Gaby up and gave her a hug — "and your poor mom. It must be killing her to be away from you. I can't even imagine."

"Well, she could come home if she wanted. I mean, she's done it before."

"Gaby, I don't want to upset you, but if your mom says it's too dangerous, then she probably knows better than any of us."

Gaby stared blankly at him. He was right. Her mom would know better than anyone. Didn't her mom used to cry whenever she talked about her first journey to the United States?

"I just want her home so bad," Gaby finally mumbled. "I miss her so much."

"Of course you do." Dr. Villalobos nodded. "Everyone needs their mom or dad. Even the dogs and cats in the shelter need their moms. Unfortunately, they get me." He shrugged. "Look, sometimes, when I have a problem, I talk to the cats. Cats have great ears for listening." Dr. V. led her out of the clinic and into the cat room. "Maybe a visit with Feather will help."

As soon as Gaby entered, Feather rushed to the front of her cage and mewed. Soon, there was a symphony of meows as all the cats sat up to greet her. Even Snowflake, who typically ignored everyone unless she wanted a ride on your shoulders, strutted over from the windowsill to rub against Gaby's leg. It was like they knew she needed them more than ever.

Gaby pulled Feather out of her cage and swayed with her like the way Dr. V. held Feather that first day at the shelter.

"Dr. V., when Cinder was adopted you whispered something to her. What did you tell her?"

From the doorway, he grinned with his whole face. "I told her that even though I'd miss her, I was happy for her, and that no matter how far away she went, she'd always be in my heart."

Gaby rubbed her face against Feather. She wished now that instead of hanging up, she had told her mom the same thing.

CHAPTER 28

The entire school day, Gaby watched Mrs. Kohler carefully for a hint that her punishment for catnapping Feather was near. During lunch and in the hallways, Gaby jumped whenever she heard Sister Joan's voice. She was sure Sister Joan was going to sneak up behind her, snag her earlobe, and drag her to the dungeon.

When the last bell of the day rang without any earlobe snagging, Gaby rushed through the hallway, weaving between students, to reach her locker, grab her books, and escape.

"Hey, speed walker," Alma yelled behind her. "Wait up!"

Gaby had just slammed her locker shut when Mrs. Kohler appeared.

"Gaby and Alma, we'd like to see you both in Sister Joan's office," she said. "Bring your things."

"But my mom is outside waiting for us," Alma said. "She's super impatient." Alma and Gaby slung their backpacks on.

"Actually . . ." Mrs. Kohler smiled. "Your mom *and* dad are with Sister Joan right now."

"Oh! Well, then, that's a relief," Alma said. "Isn't that a relief, Gaby?" Alma flashed a fake smile at Gaby. "My parents and the principal in the dungeon together. I *love* surprises like this."

"Drop the sarcasm, Alma," Mrs. Kohler warned. "And if I were you, I'd remove that scarf. Sister Joan is not feeling very lenient today."

Alma yanked off her scarf and stuffed it into her backpack. When they reached the dungeon, Alma's parents and Dr. Villalobos were already seated. Sister Joan sat behind her dark wood desk gazing at Dr. V. with a wide, laughing smile. But as soon as she saw Gaby and Alma, the warning stare came out.

"Please take a seat," she said.

Alma sat next to her mom. Gaby stood and looked around. Her father wasn't there.

"What are you doing?" Alma tapped the seat next to her. "Come sit here."

Gaby took her seat. Sister Joan faced Gaby.

"I called your father," she started. "He said he was unavailable to meet today, but he mentioned that he has found a job out of town and that you'd be moving with him. If that is the case, it's going to be a real shame for St. Ann's." Sister Joan shook her head. "I still remember the day your mom showed up at our convent so many years ago. She arrived with a bucket of cleaning supplies in one hand and you in the other. While she cleaned, you'd sing a song in Spanish and it filled our entire convent with joy." Gaby's nose tingled and she felt a lump in her throat. She remembered those days, too. Back then, she accompanied her mom to all her cleaning jobs. Now the faintest trace of lemon-scented soap brought back memories of her mom scrubbing, waxing, dusting, and mopping.

Sister Joan walked around the desk and sat at the edge of it to be closer to Gaby. Her posture was straight and proper.

"Your mom worked hard for you to be here so that you could have the best education and be surrounded with people who love you, like us. You can't forget that, Gaby."

"I won't." Gaby stared down at her hands. Now she felt even more horrible for how she had talked to her mom on the phone.

"Now, I've talked to everyone involved regarding the regrettable shenanigans with the cat. Regardless of what is going on at home — and I know it hasn't been easy — this behavior is unacceptable." Gaby lowered her head and nodded.

"However, Dr. Villalobos tells me that you saved a litter of kittens and Mrs. Kohler says that you have taken on extra work writing profiles for the animals at the shelter. They both believe you deserve a second chance, but I'd like to hear one of these profiles before I make my final decision."

Gaby grabbed her notebook from her book bag. She knew exactly which one she wanted to share. "I wrote this last night. Since I won't be able to adopt Feather . . . I wrote a profile to help her find a family." She stood and read.

FEATHER

My name is Feather. I am a young cat who has used up at least one of my nine lives. Now, I'm ready to give the rest of my lives to you. Like all great felines, I jump and pounce, and I can give you a gentle head butt when you need it, but what makes me really special is that I'm a good friend. With me, you'll never be lonely or run out of hope. I will always be at your side. Come see me at Furry Friends Animal Shelter and take me home.

Dr. V. gave her a thumbs-up.

"Feather sounds like a lovely cat," Sister Joan said. "Do you think there's a cat at the shelter that would fit in with us at the convent?"

"Yes!" Gaby leafed through the pages and stopped at Snowflake's profile. It had been difficult to write, because Snowflake was an uppity cat that ruled the shelter with a whip of her long white tail. Still, behind that tough demeanor, Gaby knew that there was a cat that wanted to be loved.

SNOWFLAKE

I am a declawed, free-roaming female feline that can keep frisky kittens and the biggest dog in check with a flick of my white whiskers and a stern meow. Because I'm an older cat, most people don't want to adopt me, but my age only means that I'm an experienced cuddler. My idea of heaven is to be carried like a fluffy cloud around your neck or to curl up on your lap while you read the newspaper. If you like to snuggle, too, make me some room and come see me at Furry Friends Animal Shelter!

Gaby looked up from her notebook to see Sister Joan's face soften into a smile.

"Gaby," Sister Joan said. "I've decided that you will not be allowed to work directly with the animals anymore."

Gaby's head dropped.

"But that's not fair!" Alma sat at the edge of her chair, ready to pounce. Her mom put her arm around Alma's shoulders. "But it's not," she mumbled. Sister Joan waited for Alma to quiet.

"As I was saying, you can't work with the animals directly," she said. "But you can still write profiles and volunteer, although you will be restricted to working with Daisy. You are not allowed to be out of her sight."

Gaby's entire body lightened. This wasn't too bad. She could handle folding newsletters, updating the website, and completing adoption papers with Daisy.

Dr. V. spoke up. "This also means no more cleaning the dog pens or cat litter boxes —"

"What?! That's not fair!" Alma cried out again. "She doesn't have to pick up dog poop?" Alma pointed her finger up. "I helped her smuggle Feather, you know. If it wasn't for me, that cat would never have made it past the bus ride."

Gaby laughed for the first time since being called into the dungeon. Mr. and Mrs. Gomez shook their heads.

Sister Joan rubbed her chin and watched Alma with amusement. "Is that so?" she said. "Consider yourself lucky,

Miss Alma. Don't think I haven't noticed the fashion liberties you've taken with your uniform as of late."

Alma sat up straight. "Yes, Sister."

With that, Sister Joan stood, shook everyone's hands, and walked them out of her office.

"No promises, but maybe I will see you ladies at the Barkapalooza open house," she said.

○ ○ ○ ○ ○ ○

Later that afternoon, Gaby stared at the phone at Alma's house. Although she was eleven years old now, she hadn't changed much from the child that Sister Joan described. She still wanted to be near her mom.

Gaby peeked into the kitchen as Alma and Mr. Gomez loaded the dishwasher.

"Mr. Gomez? Is it alright if I call my mom?"

Mr. Gomez froze. Alma nudged her dad with a spatula. "Dad, say something. Tell her yes."

"Of course, *mi hija*." He rushed over to Gaby and gave her a big hug, still holding a casserole dish.

"Dad, let her breathe!" Alma rolled her eyes.

Gaby laughed as he pulled away. "*Gracias*," she said.

In the dining room, she took a deep breath, picked up the receiver, and dialed the number. The phone rang twice before a woman answered. It wasn't her mom.

Gaby asked for her mom by name and in Spanish. "May I speak with my mom?"

"Is this Gaby?"

"Yes," Gaby answered. "Is this *Tía* Laura?"

"*Sí. Mi reina*, your mom is not here. She left to come be with you."

Gaby gasped. "What? But what about the money? Did she have enough money?"

"No, but she didn't care —" *Tía* Laura's voice broke. She coughed into the phone. "*Se fue.* She's gone, Gaby."

CHAPTER 29

In class the next morning, Gaby stared out the window. It wasn't until Alma tapped her on the shoulder that Gaby realized Mrs. Kohler was calling on her.

"Where are you, Gaby?" Mrs. Kohler asked. "Please come back to class."

Later, Gaby noticed Alma talking privately to Mrs. Kohler. After that, Mrs. Kohler stopped calling on her. No doubt she knew now that Gaby's mind was somewhere between Honduras and the United States.

Gaby spent lunch bent over her notebook at a table in the cafeteria. Alma and three of her friends hovered nearby, anxious to read Gaby's next profile. She wrote about Coco. The brown-and-white cat was "owner surrendered," which meant Coco once had a home and family, but then for some reason they had to give her up. Whenever someone entered the cat room, Coco sat up and pressed her head against the cage as if checking to see if it was her family returning for her, but it never was. It reminded Gaby of how she ran to the phone whenever it rang, hoping it was her mom calling to say she was returning home.

Now her mom was on her way home and Gaby wasn't happy; she was scared. If her mom couldn't afford a good coyote, what chance did she have to make it safely across the border? Gaby felt bad that she'd pressured her mom. She covered her face with her hands.

"Are you okay?" Alma asked.

Gaby peeked out. "Yes. I'm almost done." She ignored Alma's concerned look and wrote a few more lines before she put her pen down. She held out the notebook to Alma, who grabbed it.

"Should I read it out loud?" Alma asked.

"What? Here? Now? Are you crazy?"

"Yes to all of the above!" Alma thrust the notebook above her head like she was Moses carrying the Ten Commandments and headed straight for the stage at the far end of the cafeteria. Girls murmured as Alma passed their tables. When she reached the center of the stage, everyone hushed. Even the snobby eighth graders sitting in their corner table at the back of the cafeteria turned to see what Alma would do.

"Hi, *chicas*! As many of you know, our class volunteers at Furry Friends Animal Shelter. We invite all of you to come to our Barkapalooza open house," Alma said. "Right now, I'd like to read a short profile by Gaby Howard about one of the cats there, who desperately needs a home."

A girl yelled, "You go, *chica*!"

Gaby would recognize that voice anywhere. Liliana, Marcos's sister, sat at a table with the entire staff of the school paper. Cameras, pens, and notepads were out to record Alma's latest stunt. Liliana called for Gaby and patted the empty seat next to her. Gaby waved off the invite with a smile and moved to the back of the cafeteria. She braced herself against the wall as Alma cleared her throat and began to read.

COCO

I am a brown-and-white shorthaired cat with gold eyes. After living all my life with my family, they brought me to the shelter because they could no longer take care of me. I was sad to leave my favorite chair and the only home I've ever known. Now I am seeking a new owner that would never give me up, even when I race from the bathtub covered in suds or attack the vacuum cleaner. Are you that person? Would you promise to never leave me? Please visit Furry Friends Animal shelter and take me home today!

When she was finished, Alma looked up, searching the cafeteria until she found Gaby at the opposite end.

"Special thanks to our shelter scribe, Gaby Howard!" Alma yelled.

The cafeteria filled with applause. Dolores glanced over at Gaby, cupped her hands over her mouth, and whispered to Jan and the rest of the girls at their table. Gaby wondered why she even bothered trying to cover up her blabbering. For months, she pretended like it didn't bother her, but when a roar of laughter came from the corner table she decided enough was enough. She charged over there.

"Just for your information . . ." Gaby focused on Dolores. "My mom is risking her life to come home right now," Gaby said. Dolores and Jan glared, but Rosa looked startled. "I thought you should know in case you'd like to spread more gossip or make jokes about that."

Alma was at her side, tugging at her arm. "C'mon, Gaby. Don't waste your time on them."

Gaby let Alma pull her away. At her locker, Gaby slid down to the floor. "Did I really just go off on Dolores and Jan?"

"Yep!" Alma sat next to her, grinning. "It was awesome!"

Gaby leaned back against the locker and moaned. "What's wrong with me?"

"You stuck up for yourself. I'm thinking the dogs at the shelter are rubbing off on you."

"Great, I'm the St. Ann's stray." Gaby let out a long, deep breath. "Alma, my mom is out there because I was a big brat and didn't talk to her. If anything happens to her —" She shook her head.

"I know, Gaby." Alma put her arm around Gaby's shoulder. "I know."

CHAPTER 30

Gaby couldn't sleep. Her mother was somewhere between Honduras and Kansas. And her father's bags were packed and lined up by the front door. He'd told her that as soon as her mom got home, he'd leave for Dodge City and be out of their way. Gaby thought he seemed too eager and happy to leave. She barely spoke to him because of it.

She sat up, flipped on the light, and grabbed her notebook and pen. At the top of a blank page, she wrote "Milagro." Earlier that day, Dr. V. had sent her an e-mail that said he'd named one of the little kittens she found Milagro. It meant "miracle." And right now, a miracle was what she and her mom needed. The words poured out faster than Gaby could write, and once she finished, the phone rang. Maybe this was her miracle. She answered the phone.

"Gaby, it's *Tía* Laura."

"*Hola, Tia.* Is everything okay? Have you heard from my mom?" Gaby's father came out of his bedroom, rubbing his eyes. He sat on the recliner across from Gaby.

"*Si*, Gaby, your mom is fine, but she was tricked. She wants me to tell you she is sorry."

"Tricked? What happened? Is she okay?"

"The coyote took all her money and left her in Guatemala. All of the money is gone, but she is fine. She is on the road home."

"You mean . . ." Gaby closed her eyes and struggled to find the words in Spanish. "You mean she is heading back to *your* home?"

"Yes, Gaby. She is very sorry."

"*Gracias, Tia.*" Gaby choked back tears. "Please tell her I'm not angry." Gaby stopped. "Tell her that even though I miss her, I am happy she is safe and there to take care of you, *Tía.* She doesn't have to risk her life again because no matter how far away she is, she's in my heart always."

Gaby set the phone down.

"Is she all right?" her father asked.

"She was robbed," Gaby said softly. "She's not coming home."

Her father stood up, walked over, and took the phone from her hand. Gaby didn't resist. "No more sleeping with the phone, okay?" He returned the phone back to its charger on the table. "What do you want to do now, kiddo?" He sat down on the recliner across from her and wiped his hand over his face. He looked worried.

"Even though I knew it would be dangerous, a part of me was happy that she was finally coming home. All of this is my fault." Hot tears poured down her cheeks.

"That's not true, Gaby. None of this is your fault. Were you the one that raided the factory three months ago and had your mom arrested and deported?"

Gaby shook her head. "No."

"Were you the coyote that robbed her?"

"No."

"That's right. None of this is your fault. You're just an eleven-year-old kid that wants her mom home. There's nothing wrong with that." He stood up. "I want to show you something." He walked back to his bedroom.

Gaby grabbed her pillow and pulled it close to her. She was confused. Her father had never been this thoughtful before. What did he want to show her?

He came back out holding a folded piece of paper. He unfolded it and handed it to her.

It was the profile she'd written for herself at Alma's house. It must have slipped out of her notebook.

GABY RAMIREZ HOWARD

Just call me the St. Ann's stray. Three months ago, my mom was deported, and now I live with my father, who looks at me like I'm just another job he wants to quit. I'm seeking a home where I can invite my best friend over, and have a warm breakfast a couple times a week. Waffles and scrambled eggs are my favorite! Having the newest cell phone or fancy clothes isn't important, but I'd like to have a cat that I can talk to when I'm home alone. Come visit me at Furry Friends Animal Shelter and take me home today!

"I'm a lousy dad." He picked his fingernails.

"No." She searched for the right words. "That was just for fun." Gaby was sorry he had found the profile. She hadn't meant to hurt him.

"On the way to the shelter, you were right," he said. "I haven't spent enough time at home with you. I guess mostly because I didn't know how to take care of you or what you needed from me, but — I am proud of you." He ran a hand through his hair. "You deserve everything you wrote in that profile. Every single thing. And, well, I don't have to tell you, I guess, but . . . I suck at being a dad. I can't give you those things, but I know a family that wants to."

"Alma's family." Gaby exhaled. Her father nodded. "So, I don't have to go to Dodge City? I can live with Alma's family?"

"They love you, Gaby. And it's about time you got what you want for a change, right?"

"Thank you, Dad!" She felt like she had been trapped in a closed room for months and someone had finally opened a window. She rushed up to hug him. After a few seconds, she felt him hug her back.

Chapter 31

The next day, Gaby, with Alma's help, filled up two trash bags and her book bag with every single belonging she owned in the world. Her dad and Mr. Gomez finished loading his truck.

Outside, Gaby's dad handed the house keys to Mr. Gomez, and then they piled Gaby's bags into Mr. Gomez's car.

Gaby's dad gave her a long hug. "I'll call once I'm settled."

Her father climbed into the truck, waved, and then pulled away from the curb. She waved until his truck turned the corner. She hoped with all her heart that the job would work out for him and that he would remember to call.

Mr. Gomez put his arm around Gaby's shoulder. "Once I lock the door, *hija*, I have to take the keys to the owner. Do you want to take a few minutes?"

She faced the house. It was the smallest on the block. Her mom had painted it light yellow to remind her of the "Honduran sun." In this way, she said, she would always be at home.

Gaby walked up the porch steps and into the house. The couch she'd slept on every night since her mom left, two mattresses, the dining room table and chairs, and the phone she slept next to night after night were all that remained. She touched the phone one last time.

"*Adios*, house." Gaby walked out and shut the door. On the porch, she grabbed the little white saucer and stuffed it into her pocket.

"Are you sad?" Alma asked.

"It hasn't felt like my home since my mom left." Gaby shrugged, then smiled. "If Dr. V. was here right now, you know what he'd say?"

"He'd say, 'You're one lucky girl to be living with Alma Gomez.'"

"Not even close. He'd say, 'You're off to a brand-new start on life . . .'"

"'. . . isn't that phenomenal?'" Alma finished. She threw her hands up and shook them around. She was still strutting around with her crazy hands when Mr. Gomez opened the car door and called them. Gaby took a long look at her home. It was all happening so fast.

"Is it okay if we walk home?" Gaby asked. Alma locked arms with her and they walked like that all the way home.

o   o   o   o   o   o

That evening at Alma's house, Gaby's mother called. Between sobs, Gaby apologized and told her she didn't want her to risk her life trying to return to the States. It wasn't worth it. They were lucky this time. If her mom tried again, it could be worse. She also told her about Feather.

"I think you took that cat because you missed me," her mom said. "You were trying to save it the same way you tried to save me from being deported. I remember how you'd come with your rosary when I was detained. You told everyone that would listen how you were my daughter and that you wanted me home."

Gaby shook her head. "Yeah, but it didn't help. I haven't saved anyone. Feather is back at the shelter and you're still far away."

"Everything's going to be all right, *princesa*," her mom said. "Do you know what? The whole time I was walking through Honduras, I'd see stray dogs, and I thought of what

194

you might write about them. I even gave them silly names like Pepito, Gordo, Suerte, or Flaco . . . It helped me not be so scared. Could you read me another animal story?"

Gaby swallowed hard. She could only imagine how frightened her mom must have been after being deserted in Guatemala. She pulled out her notebook and found Milagro's profile.

MILAGRO

My name is Spanish for "miracle." I was named this because it was a miracle that someone found me and my siblings when we were abandoned and only a few days old. When I was found, my eyes were shut, but now they are wide open and I can see everything: yellow flowers, balls of yarn, saucers of milk, and especially your face. Because I am so teeny-tiny, I need to stay at the shelter with my siblings for a while, but if you're willing to wait, please visit me at Furry Friends Animal Shelter and sign up to be my forever family!

"*Ay*, Gaby, that is beautiful!" Then, she was suddenly silent.

"Mom, are you still there?"

"*Estoy aqui*. I was just thinking . . . maybe someday you can come visit me in Honduras? Would you like that? Maybe together we could help the stray animals here?"

Gaby's heart danced. "I would love that."

"Only thing is . . . I think if you visited me in Honduras, you'd miss Marcos too much."

"No way!" Gaby shrieked. "I wouldn't miss him at all!"

"I don't know, I remember how you always said he was cute —"

"No way!" Gaby shook her head and screamed till she laughed.

"We'll see, *mi princesa*. Remember, I'm your mom. I know you very well."

Gaby pulled her knees up to her chest and held the phone closer. For so long, she had felt like a cat stuck in a tree, peering down and crying out. Now her mom's voice was carrying her through the branches and safely back down to the ground.

CHAPTER 32

"Roll over, Spike!" Alma ordered. The small dog dropped and rolled over. From a bench, Gaby and Daisy watched Alma lead Spike through various drills. Daisy held Feather on her lap. It was her way to let Gaby spend time with the cat. Gaby was grateful. Feather's owners still hadn't showed up, and it was looking more and more like they'd never return. And as long as Daisy was around, Gaby was allowed a break from copying and filing to go outside and watch the dogs train.

"Now for the finale!" Alma extended her right hand in front of Spike. "Stay, Spike. Stay!" Spike's tail wagged and his ears perked up, but he stayed seated. Alma walked away.

Daisy nudged Gaby with her elbow. "Is he really going to stay this time?"

When Alma took a few more steps Spike darted past her and then circled her.

"Noooooo!" Alma covered her face with her hands. "What was that? Ten seconds, maybe?"

"Don't give up, Alma," Daisy said. "He's improved 99.9 percent since he first arrived here."

Alma dropped down on the grass. Spike sat across from her until he saw Atticus running loose and decided it was a good idea to chase a dog twice as big and three times as heavy as he was. Alma collapsed flat on the ground. Her hands beckoned the heavens. "He's crazy!"

Spike tackled Atticus and was now gnawing on the poor shepherd's neck. Atticus kept trying to swipe the small dog off with his paws, but Spike eluded each strike.

"How can that small creature scare all those big dogs like that?" Daisy smirked.

"Are you talking about Spike or Alma?" Gaby asked. Daisy laughed.

Just then, Dr. V. came outside with a man and woman. He was pointing at the dogs scattered throughout the yard. Daisy passed Feather to Gaby and joined Dr. V.

Spike let Atticus escape. He swaggered over to Alma and dropped his toy panda at her feet.

"A saliva-drenched stuffed panda! You shouldn't have!" Alma grabbed Spike's gift with the tip of her fingers. It used to be a plush panda bear, but now its ears were chewed off and it was missing an eye.

"Poor little bear! He needs a shelter of his own," Gaby said.

Alma swung the bear in front of him. Spike pawed and lunged at it.

Gaby watched as Daisy, Dr. V., and the couple moved around the yard. They squatted down to pet the dogs. "They're making eye contact with the dogs; that's good."

"Who?" Alma asked.

"That couple." The man pulled out a flyer from his jacket pocket and handed it to Dr. Villalobos. "He has one of my flyers." From across the yard, Dr. Villalobos met Gaby's eyes with a worried look. Gaby hugged Feather closer to her chest.

Spike jerked the toy panda away from Alma just as Dr. Villalobos and the couple approached. He chomped on the panda's remaining eye.

"Alma, this is Martin and Sylvia; they're interested in adopting today," Dr. Villalobos said.

Dr. V. handed the flyer to Alma. It was Spike's flyer. Gaby gasped. Alma gave it back to Dr. Villalobos. She didn't

need to read it. Gaby had read the flyer to her a dozen times.
She'd wanted to get Spike just right. And she did.

SPIKE

Hi, my name is Spike! I am a small black-and-white terrier mix that loves tug-of-war and my stuffed panda. I also enjoy breakfast, lunch, and dinner. I was brought in by my former family because they thought I was too wild. Since coming to the shelter, I've learned to channel my energy into tricks! If you have friends over for dinner, I can shake their hands and roll over for them. My only dislikes are fleas, empty water bowls, and rainy days when I can't go outside and chase squirrels! Visit Furry Friends Animal Shelter and take a chance on me!

"Do you want to show them the tricks he's learned?" Dr. Villalobos asked.

Alma exchanged a nervous glance with Gaby. "All right." She clapped and called Spike. He dropped the stuffed panda and barked. "Sit, Spike, sit!" she ordered. Alma's face became tense and her booming voice lowered. Spike immediately sat up, with his tail wagging happily.

"Silly dog," Gaby whispered to Feather. "Doesn't he know they're going to take him away from Alma?"

"Roll over!" Spike dropped and rolled over in perfect form. The woman squeezed her husband's arm and laughed.

"Isn't that fantastic?" Dr. Villalobos grinned.

"Shake hands." Spike lifted his paw and Alma gently shook it. The couple nodded approvingly. Alma looked up at the couple. "Well, that's what he's learned so far —"

The couple's eyes widened. Gaby knew that look. She had seen those same glowing eyes and approving smiles from other folks who came to the shelter and then walked out with a pet. She stepped forward.

"There's one more trick," she called out. "You need to show them how he can 'stay,' remember?"

Daisy and Dr. V. gave Gaby a confused look.

"That's right." Alma narrowed her eyes at Gaby. "Give me one minute." Alma pulled Gaby away from the group.

Spike followed them, which made everyone laugh. "What are you doing?"

"If Spike doesn't stay put and starts one of his crazy tantrums," Gaby whispered to her, "they won't want a lunatic dog, right?"

Alma gazed down at Spike. His ears were perked up and his tail thumped against the ground. He was waiting for his next instruction. "But doesn't he deserve a good home? Maybe they are the ones who will love him forever."

"But you'll lose him, Alma."

"I know . . . you're right. Why did you have to write such a cute profile for him?" She pouted at Gaby before turning back to everyone.

"I wish I hadn't," Gaby mumbled to herself.

"Okay, one more trick," Alma announced. She bent down and extended her right palm in front of Spike. He looked up at her with wet brown eyes, and for a minute she didn't say anything. She stayed there and stared at Spike with loving eyes.

"Alma?" Dr. V. asked. A few of the other girls giggled, and Gaby flashed them a look that said, "Don't you dare laugh!"

"Oh!" Alma flushed. She straightened her posture and put out her right hand. "Stay, Spike! Stay!" She walked away.

Gaby felt her heart sink. Feather mewed. Spike sat completely still. He wasn't pulling on Alma's pant leg or attacking her shoes. In fact, he was sitting right where Alma had left him. He was staying. After several more steps, Alma turned around.

"Wow," she said. "The little rascal finally did it." Spike opened his mouth and showed all his teeth. All the girls who had fallen trying to hold Spike down applauded. This, they knew, was a major achievement.

Even as the girls cheered and the couple talked excitedly back and forth, Spike never moved.

"Good dog! Come here, Spike!" Alma clapped and Spike ran to her. She dropped down on the ground and hugged him. "That's a good dog! Yes, you are!" He licked her face.

"We think he's perfect for us; we'll take him!" the man said.

All of the girls moaned. Gaby buried her head into Feather's soft fur as Alma kissed Spike's ear and whispered to him. She heard her friend say, "I love you, sweet Spike."

ChAPTeR 33

After the couple left in their Volkswagen with Spike, Dr. Villalobos put his arm around Alma and tried to cheer all the girls up. "Think of it like this — now, instead of sleeping in a cage with newspaper and an old blanket, Spike will have a real home."

Alma folded her arms across her chest and walked out of the shelter. Gaby followed her onto the bus, and they stayed there until the rest of girls and Mrs. Kohler joined them for the ride back to school.

It was a quiet trip. Every girl was upset by Spike's

departure. Alma sat in the back of the small bus, head against the window, with her knees drawn up to her chest. Gaby sat across from her in the same row and watched the tears stream down her best friend's cheek.

As soon as the girls arrived home, Alma ran upstairs and locked the bedroom door behind her. Gaby sat downstairs at the kitchen table across from Alma's mom. Both of them tried to remember a time when they had ever seen Alma so upset.

"There was one time when all the kids were running through the sprinklers in Marcos's backyard and Alma stepped on a piece of glass," Gaby offered. "She cried a little then."

Mrs. Gomez groaned. A trip to the emergency room and a dozen stitches later, Alma was back to her sassy self.

"We joke about that day now, you know," Gaby said. "Alma tells Marcos, 'The way you were blubbering, you'd think it was you who sliced up your foot.' And he always says, 'It was like a war zone with all that blood splatter. It freaked me out.' And then Alma calls him a big crybaby."

Alma's mom laughed. "Marcos and Alma, they are like salt and pepper." Alma's mom had the best laugh. It was a laugh that reminded Gaby of when the music teacher at school played the scales on the piano. It was nice being in a home where people laughed. And ever since she'd moved in with the Gomezes, Gaby found herself laughing more, too.

Now, everyone in the neighborhood knew that Gaby was a permanent member of the Gomez family, and it felt good to her. Every Friday was movie night and Saturdays they went to the library to study. Gaby had checked out a book on Honduras. Soon, the animal profiles were not the only things that filled Gaby's notebook. In between the profiles, she wrote questions about Honduras to ask her mom. She wanted to know about a street food called a *baleada*, the Mayan pyramids in Copán Ruinas, the exotic Roatán Island, and an indigenous people called the Garifuna. Mrs. Gomez even checked out a Honduran cookbook so they could learn some recipes. Gaby was grateful to have a home and a family where her fascination with Honduras was encouraged.

"So that's the last time you've seen Alma cry, huh?" Mrs. Gomez got up from the table and gave Gaby a kiss on the top of her head. "Well, now that you two are under one roof, I hope to hear more laughing than crying."

Then, just like that, Gaby remembered the *real* last time she had seen Alma cry. It was the day Mrs. Gomez had picked the girls up from school early to tell them that Gaby's mom had been arrested at work. Alma wept immediately. She seemed to know what it meant before Gaby could even grasp Mrs. Gomez's words. Two weeks later, when her mom was deported, Gaby cried for a week straight. It was Alma who finally dragged her outside and back into the world.

Gaby had to return the favor.

She went upstairs and stood outside the bedroom door. She could hear Alma crying softly inside. She tapped on the door. "I have a new profile, Alma." Gaby could hear Alma's bed rattling as her friend pulled herself up. She opened her bedroom door. Alma's eyes were red and puffy. Gaby sat on the floor and Alma slid down next to her. "I finished the profile for Atticus." Gaby read it aloud.

ATTICUS

My name is Atticus. I am a three-year-old shepherd mix. I was transferred to Furry Friends Animal Shelter with my best buddy, Finch. Finch and I've been together for years and we'd like to stay together forever. If you have a big yard and would like to make two dogs really happy, we'd love to be with the same family. We'd bring a double dose of fun to your home! Some of our favorite things are dog biscuits, bowls full of cold water, chasing birds, and playing fetch. If you think you can keep up with us, come visit Furry Friends Animal Shelter today and take me (and Finch!) home!

"It's beautiful," Alma said. "Atticus and Finch should always stay together." She wiped her eyes with her sleeve.

"Like us," Gaby added.

Alma nodded and held Gaby's hand like they used to when they were in kindergarten. "It's weird, you know? Our number one goal at the shelter has been to get all the animals adopted and yet when it happened with Spike . . . I wanted him to be unadoptable. I didn't want to lose him. Some Furry Friend I am."

"You loved him," Gaby said. "And in the end you did the right thing. Unlike me with Feather."

"But Feather's owners weren't nice. That's different."

"Maybe." Gaby shrugged. "Still, I'm going to have to say good-bye to Feather someday."

Alma let out a heavy breath and wiped her eyes. "I miss Spike so much."

Gaby opened her arms wide. "Have you ever had an eraser hug?"

"A what?"

"I used to give them to my mom all the time. Here, come closer."

Alma backed away. "Is this going to hurt?"

"C'mon, Alma."

Alma scooted closer. Gaby closed her arms around her until the eraser hug took over and neither one of them could stop giggling.

Chapter 34

On the last day at the shelter, Gaby and her classmates buzzed from one cat and dog to another, kissing farewells. Cameras zoomed in and out, flashed and clicked to capture whiskers, ears, muzzles, and paws forever.

"We are the puppyrazzi!" Alma shouted.

Dr. Villalobos came out of the shelter, lugging a camera and tripod. He didn't wear his usual blue jeans, T-shirt, and sneakers. Today, he was dressed to impress in khaki chinos, a blue polo shirt, and loafers. "Group meeting!" he yelled. Gaby liked that he hadn't gone with a long-sleeve shirt to cover his tattoos or removed the silver stud from his ear. The clothes were more formal, but he was still Dr. Villalobos. The girls gathered around him. "Daisy's got good news!"

Daisy stepped forward. "This past weekend, Atticus and Finch were adopted by a nice family, who has three little boys and lots of land. They'll be here today to take Atticus and Finch home." All the girls squealed and clapped. "It seems Gaby's flyer did the trick again. Great job, kiddo!" She gave Gaby a salute. "And a lady who moved here from Albuquerque is planning to come tomorrow to adopt Puck. How's that for a great beginning to our Barkapalooza open house?"

Dr. V. stood in the center of the group, as silent as any of the girls had seen him. "I am really going to miss you," he said. "So before our guests arrive, I want to let you know that this is the last time you'll ever see me in a polo shirt." Everyone laughed. "Would you honor me with a group picture?"

While Daisy corralled Atticus and Finch, the girls lined up to pose with a pet of their choice. Gaby held Feather. Alma took the new kitten Milagro. Secret nestled in Mrs. Kohler's arms. Dr. Villalobos sat in the center with Snowflake on his shoulder and Puck on his lap. Daisy set the camera's timer and rushed over to join the group. "Say 'kitties,' everyone!" she shouted.

After the picture, the girls scattered to make final preparations before guests arrived. While some girls set up the refreshment table with cookies and punch, others unfolded chairs on the lawn. As part of the welcoming committee, Gaby and Alma sorted through name tags and brochures with Daisy at the entrance.

Sister Joan and a flock of nuns from school were the first to arrive. For several days now, there had been rumors that Sister Joan planned to adopt Snowflake. As soon as she appeared, several girls ran to find Dr. Villalobos, because they were 100 percent sure that Snowflake was still draped around his neck. Behind the nuns, a group of eighth graders slinked in like alley cats. Gaby was happy to see that Dolores and Jan were not among them. Their lip-glossed mouths gaped open as they took in the shelter's big backyard. Gaby was forced to welcome them because she was one of the only greeters who hadn't run off to find Snowflake. Alma stayed close.

"Thank you for coming to our open house!" Gaby said. "Would you like some punch?"

The girls looked at one another and laughed. Gaby froze. Alma charged forward.

"Hey, if you don't want punch, that's fine, but don't be rude," she snapped. The laughing stopped. "Especially you, Rosa!" Alma pointed. "My mom knows your mom! And she would not be cool with how you, Dolores, and Jan have been treating Gaby!" Rosa winced and stepped back as if Alma had threatened to confiscate all her lip gloss.

"It's okay, Alma." Gaby waved Alma off. She straightened her shoulders and looked Rosa in the eye. "There are animals here that need homes. If you think that's funny, laugh all you want, but don't waste my time."

Rosa shook her head. "No, no, we weren't laughing at you," she said. Her light brown eyes lowered and then she looked directly at Gaby. "Really, we weren't. We laughed because all day Dolores kept saying how lame this thing was going to be, but as usual she was wrong." A smile spread across her face. "This is way cooler than our stupid clean-up-the-park day." Her friends mumbled agreement. "And I happen to love punch."

"So, then, you're not here to make fun?" Gaby asked.

"No way." She shook her head. "I've always stood up for you because . . . well, besides the fact that Dolores and Jan are certifiable idiots" — all of her friends nodded — "it's not right." Her voice softened. "My cousin was deported around the same time as your mom. We haven't heard from him since." Rosa's voice choked.

"I'm sorry, I didn't know that." Gaby's heart sank. She knew that feeling.

"That day in the cafeteria you said your mom was coming back. Did she make it?"

"No, but she's okay."

"Good, I'm glad. Anyway, I wanted you to know that

you're not alone." Then Rosa shook herself like a delicate bird stepping out of a bath. She turned and pointed at Alma. "And you, Miss Thang! Dolores and Jan are scared of you. Do you even know that?"

Alma shrugged. "I have that effect on certifiable idiots."

Rosa giggled and looped her arm through Alma's like they were long-lost BFFs. "So where's the punch?" As Alma led Rosa and her posse to the refreshment table, Gaby stood still, stunned. All this time, there were actually eighth graders at St. Ann's that didn't want to make her life miserable. And not just any eighth grader, but Rosa Solis! She was the queen of the eighth graders. Gaby would have stayed frozen longer had Cinder not jumped on her and licked her entire face. "Oh! My shy girl, Cinder!" Cinder wore a pink bandana tied around her neck. The firemen gathered around and gave Gaby big hugs before they moved on to the refreshment table.

As more parents and pet owners arrived, some toured the shelter while others mingled near the refreshments. Gaby introduced Chloe from the coffee shop to the couple that had adopted Willow. Chloe was there to adopt Pouncer and wanted tips on organic cat food. A few minutes later, Gaby felt a tug on her sleeve. Three small, redheaded, freckle-faced boys gazed up at her. "We brought treats for Atticus and Finch," they said.

"Treats! Treats!" the smallest boy repeated. Above them hovered a mom and dad just as redheaded and freckled. They reminded her of a patch of strawberries.

"Oh, Atticus and Finch told me to take you to them as soon as you arrived. They are so excited!" Gaby held out her hands and the boys quickly grabbed ahold and walked with her toward Atticus and Finch's cage.

While punch glasses were refilled and a second batch of cookies was brought out, Alma's parents arrived with Marcos and Enrique. The boys had lawn chairs flung over their shoulders.

"So this is Dead Furry Friends Animal Shelter, huh?" Marcos nudged Alma. She nudged him back and almost knocked him to the ground.

Dr. V. waved Alma's parents over.

"What are they doing?" Gaby watched them enter the shelter with Dr. Villalobos. "The presentation is going to start soon." Alma put her arm around Gaby's shoulder and steered her attention back to Marcos, who had already introduced himself to Rosa and was reading her palm.

A few minutes later, Dr. V. was at the microphone. "Thank you for coming!" he roared. Gaby and Alma joined Mrs. Kohler and their classmates on the lawn. "Welcome to our Barkapalooza open house." Then, for the second time that afternoon, Dr. V. was quiet. He gazed at all the girls.

"When Mrs. Kohler approached me about a school service project, I'd thought it'd be cool, but it turned out to be huge! Together we've learned that animals depend on us to take care of them." He winked at Gaby. "I hope all of you will be my furry friends forever." Everyone clapped. "Now, let me introduce the Jedi Master of dog training. If you have a dog that can roll over and sit and stay, it's probably because of Alma. From what I understand, she also has that power over the boys on her block!" Marcos and Enrique shook their heads. "Alma Gomez!" Dr. V. yelled. Alma walked to the front as the crowd applauded.

"Thanks!" she said. "Please sit and stay!"

The crowd laughed. "I'd like to recognize our team of trainers. Please stand, *chicas*!" Gaby was always amazed at Alma's ability to speak in front of crowds. There were no "ums" or "you knows." As Alma called out their names, each girl waved, blew kisses, or did fist pumps. "Last, but not least, I'd like to recognize Gaby Ramirez Howard, who wrote all of the profiles for our flyers and website."

Gaby stood and waved. It was her first real glimpse of everyone who had arrived. Chloe sat in a lawn chair with Pouncer on her lap. The strawberry family had Atticus and Finch. Snowflake was draped around Sister Joan's neck. Cinder was getting her ears rubbed by the firemen at her side. Even her classmates had at least one parent present. Every family seemed complete. It made her wish for her mom and Feather. She looked toward the cat room. Maybe she could grab Feather really fast? Then things would be 99 percent complete. Not 100 percent, because there was still one hyper little black-and-white terrier missing. Spike hadn't arrived yet.

"We will read a few samples of Gaby's profiles," Alma said. While Daisy stood to read Finch's profile, one of the redheaded boys yelled, "She's reading about Finch!"

Next, Mrs. Kohler read Puck's profile. Gaby noticed that during the reading, Alma strained her neck to see the entrance. Gaby caught her eye. Alma smiled and shrugged. Gaby closed her eyes and prayed. "Please show up, Spike."

When Mrs. Kohler finished, it was Dr. V.'s turn. He stood up and began to read. "Hi, my name is Feather, and I'm a cute tabby . . ."

Gaby sucked in her breath. What was going on? Why was Dr. V. reading Feather's profile?

". . . I was abandoned at a rest stop by an evil couple, but now I am healthy and safe . . ."

That wasn't Feather's profile! Gaby glanced over at Alma, who stood there with a big goofy grin. What was going on? Did this mean that the awful couple wasn't coming back for Feather?

". . . I am ready for a new adventure and excited about living with Gaby and the entire Gomez family!"

Dr. Villalobos stopped. Now, all of Gaby's classmates were looking at her with the same goofy smile Alma had on her face. Mr. Gomez stood next to Dr. V., holding Feather. Alma ran to Gaby and dragged her to the front. "C'mon, Gaby!"

"Gaby, in special gratitude for your tireless work as our shelter scribe," Dr. V. began, "you are now the proud forever family of Feather!" Dr. V. took Feather from Mr. Gomez and handed the cat to her.

"What? I don't understand . . ." Gaby stammered. "What about those people? Are you sure?"

"They never came back and I told you that you were on the waiting list. So . . ." Dr. V. smiled. "She's all yours!"

Gaby's hands trembled as she took Feather from Dr. V. She couldn't believe this was happening. She looked over at Alma and Alma's parents to see if it was true. Their smiles confirmed it was real. Feather nuzzled up against Gaby's cheek and meowed. "You're right, Feather," Gaby whispered. "We're not strays anymore."

ChapteR 35

Gaby had just given Dr. V. a hug when she saw a flash of black and white at the entrance out of the corner of her eye.

"It's Spike!" Gaby shouted. The guests turned to find the source of the commotion.

Alma bolted and wrapped her arms around Spike. Soon all the girls were on their knees huddled around him, too. Spike barked and slobbered them with kisses. The whole time his tail wagged like he was swatting flies.

"He smells so good!" Alma gushed. The girls buried their noses into his fur and nodded.

"It's the organic shampoo we use. Animal-friendly stuff," the woman said, brushing blond bangs away from her green eyes. "Sorry we're late."

"Spike has arrived," Dr. Villalobos announced over the microphone. "Please be sure to watch your punch and cookies! Thanks for coming, everyone!"

After the guests left, Dr. Villalobos and Daisy walked the girls to the parking lot and hugged each girl good-bye.

"Don't forget to howl every once in a while," he said as the girls walked to their parents' cars. All of the girls turned around and answered with screams and howls. Dr. V. laughed and gave a thumbs-up. "That's what I'm talking about."

Marcos opened the car door for Gaby. "He seems like a cool dude."

"The coolest," she said. The four kids crowded into the backseat. Feather rested on Marcos's lap. She purred while he absently scratched her behind the ears. As they drove away, Gaby looked back to see Dr. V., still waving good-bye. She missed him already.

"Hey, slug bug!" Enrique slugged Gaby in the arm.

"Ouch! Where did you see the slug bug?" She rubbed her arm. "I didn't see one."

"It's right there. The one with that Spike dog you all were slobbering over earlier."

"Spike?" Gaby and Alma said at the same time. The girls looked out and saw Spike with his head out the back window of an orange Volkswagen bug driving alongside them, a lane over.

Alma rolled down the window and yelled out, "Bye, Spike!"

Spike barked and his owners waved before taking a right turn.

"Why do dogs stick their heads out like that?" Marcos asked.

"It means they're happy," Alma answered. "If you were happy, wouldn't you want to stick your head out a window?"

Feather looked up at Gaby from Marcos's lap and mewed, as if saying, "Go ahead." Gaby lowered her window. She couldn't wait to tell her mom that Feather was now a permanent member of their family. Her mom would do the happy dance for sure.

Gaby closed her eyes and stuck her head out into the wind. The warm breeze blew her hair back, as the sun's rays pressed against her smiling face.